Stevi's eyes widened as she drew closer and closer to the form that had been washed ashore.

Her breath had somehow gotten stuck in her throat. There was no longer a question in her mind what she was looking at. The clump of seaweed had somehow managed to turn into the very real form of a man.

A man lying still and facedown in the sand.

She didn't remember how the last fifteen feet were reduced to less than a foot. Couldn't remember if she ran toward the prone body or if she approached it cautiously. Given her usual recklessness, she probably ran, Stevi thought.

But suddenly, there she was, standing over the immobile body of a man, wondering if he was dead or just unconscious.

"Mister?"

Dear Reader,

So, we meet again. This time, it's for Stephanie's story. Stevi is Richard's third daughter, the artistic, creative one who, just possibly, has given him the most concern. As Stevi's formal education comes to a close and she graduates college, she finds herself growing more and more restless. Still undecided where she will wind up going—New York City? Paris? Or…? She takes to channeling some of her energy into early morning runs along the beach. This particular early morning, she finds more than just a seashell in her path. She comes across a man who has washed up on the beach and is half dead, thanks to the wound in his chest.

Thinking only that she has to save this man's life, Stevi enlists the help of the inn's gardener, a man with a mysterious past who came to work for her father some fifteen years earlier. Silvio brings the unconscious man back to the inn and patches him up.

As she nurses her stranger back to health, Stevi finds herself more and more enamored with the man who claims to have no memory of the events that brought him to her beach. By the time he's well enough to leave, she fervently hopes he doesn't. But he is just as determined to go before his past catches up to him—and hurts the family he has come to care so much about.

I hope you stay to find out how it all turns out. And if you do, as always, I thank you for reading, and from the bottom of my heart, I wish you someone to love who loves you back.

All the best,

Marie Ferrarella

HARLEQUIN HEARTWARMING

USA TODAY Bestselling Author

Marie Ferrarella

Safe Harbor

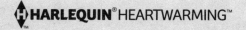
HARLEQUIN® HEARTWARMING™

Recycling programs
for this product may
not exist in your area.

ISBN-13: 978-0-373-36679-8

SAFE HARBOR

HARLEQUIN®
™ www.Harlequin.com

Printed in U.S.A.

MARIE FERRARELLA

is a *USA TODAY* bestselling and RITA® Award-winning author, and has written more than 240 books for Harlequin, some under the name Marie Nicole. As of January 2013, she has been published by Harlequin for 30 years. She earned a master's degree in Shakespearean comedy and, perhaps as a result, her writing is distinguished by humor and natural dialogue. Her goal is to entertain and to make people laugh and feel good. Her romances are beloved by fans worldwide. Visit her website, www.marieferrarella.com.

To
Victoria Curran
for giving me
a really great
suggestion

PROLOGUE

THE USUAL JUNE-GLOOM weather was happily absent from the scene despite the fact that it was barely eight in the morning. A light breeze was drifting in from the ocean, bringing just a faint touch of moisture to the modest family cemetery.

Richard Roman had made his usual pilgrimage down the hill from Ladera-by-the-Sea, the family bed-and-breakfast inn he owned and ran, with the help of his daughters, to the small family cemetery where, among others, his wife and his best friend, Dan Taylor, were buried.

It was his custom to come here to share his thoughts, his feelings and any news that might be unfolding in the sedate, yet ever-changing world of the one-hundred-and-twenty-year-old inn.

Richard felt as if he were still in touch with his Amy and with Dan, if he came here, to stand between their headstones.

He dearly loved all four of his daughters and regarded Alex's and Cris's husbands, Wyatt and Shane, as if they were his own sons, but the two people he had felt closest to were both here, resting beneath the warm earth, waiting for the day when he could come and join them. The family he lived with at the inn had his heart, but Dan and especially Amy had his soul and he was never quite whole except when he was here, at the cemetery with them.

"Stevi graduated yesterday," he announced, looking down at Amy's white marble headstone. "I wish you could have been there, you would have been so proud. I would have loved to have held your hand in mine, actually *held* it, when Stevi marched across that stage to get her diploma." He chuckled. "I half expected her to do a cartwheel across the stage. She's been really dying to graduate." He paused, reflecting sadly on that. "Now she says there's nothing stopping her from going off and following her dreams."

Richard sighed. "She's talking about going to New York, Amy, or somewhere equally exciting."

He looked down at Dan's headstone. "You were always going somewhere, following the next story, the next lead. I always figured you were half journalist, half nomad. If it wasn't for your summers here with Wyatt, I don't think I would have seen you even half as much as I did." He laughed, shaking his head. "This is the longest you've ever stayed put anywhere."

He looked off toward the ocean, watching the waves rise and chase one another to the shore. It soothed him a little.

"Maybe I'm hopelessly old-fashioned, but I feel it's different for a girl, different going off on her own. Sure, I'd also worry if this was my son, but you tend to want to protect a daughter, even if she has a scissor tongue and is pretty resourceful, like Stevi. If either of you two can come up with a way I can get her to stay here, I'd really appreciate it," he said, spreading his arms helplessly.

"Oh, I almost forgot. Stevi has me all turned around," he apologized. "Guess what?"

Holding on to his big news for a moment longer, Richard looked from one grave site to the other. "Okay, okay, I won't torture you with this." His grin grew twice as wide when he said, "Guess who's going to be a grandparent?" His own words echoed back to him and he laughed. "I guess I didn't really phrase that right because all three of us are." He could barely contain his joy as he said, "Alex and Wyatt are expecting. It'll be a Christmas baby unless I miscalculated. And if this new little person has half the energy that Alex had at that age, I'd say that Alex and Wyatt are in big trouble."

He sat down on the rim of the seat that Shane, his other son-in-law, had built into the base of the pine tree overlooking these two graves.

"You have no idea what I wouldn't give to be able to see you holding our second grandchild, Amy. Or you, for that matter," he added with a laugh as he glanced over toward Dan's grave. "I can still remember you with Wyatt. He was so little and you looked like a fish out of water. A big and awkward fish. But to your credit, you didn't drop him, not once. Still, I think, if you were here and it was your turn to hold this new person on the way into our lives, I'd insist you sit down first—just in case."

Richard glanced at his wristwatch—the one Amy had given him on their wedding day—and rose. "I'd better be getting back. It's time to get things rolling. Alex is still running things, but I'm trying to get her to relax a little, make her realize that she has nothing to prove anymore. That's our Alex, though. Always looking for challenges to vanquish.

"Don't forget what I asked you two to do," he said by way of parting. "Find a way—a *good* way, to get our Stevi to want to stay right here, close to home. We need her and even though she might not realize it, she needs us.

"I'll be back as soon as I can," he promised. "You know I can hardly let a day go by without visiting with you two, unless something pressing keeps me away."

With a smile curving the corners of his mouth, Richard squared his shoulders and headed back up the hill. The inn—and his family—were waiting for him.

It was nice, Richard couldn't help thinking, to be needed.

CHAPTER ONE

SHE WAS AWARE of the dull ache in her calf muscles as they tensed with each footfall while she ran, for the most part, parallel to the shoreline.

Waves flowed in, then ebbed away, sometimes drenching her up to the ankles. Stephanie Roman hardly noticed. She kept her mind focused on her goal, reaching the sand dune whimsically shaped like a cave for vertically challenged elves.

Stevi, as her family had always called her, was fairly new to this concept of getting regular exercise. She'd undertaken running a few short months ago as a way of channeling her energy.

Once begun, however, she found this form of exercise addictive, a realization that took her completely by surprise. But even as she craved it, running to her was a chore, something she needed to mark off on her to-do checklist before she could continue, unobstructed, with the rest of her day.

She didn't realize that she was addicted to it until, overwhelmed with work, she tried skipping a run and found herself feeling utterly out of sync with her own body.

Less than a month ago, she had been juggling classes, a part-time job—she helped out at the inn—and her artwork. She created many of the paintings that hung in the rooms in her family's inn.

A select few of her works of art were on the walls of a local art gallery.

They represented her start.

Now that college and her classes were finally part of her past, with a degree in art to show for it, Stevi's time was freed up somewhat. Except she was still out here, on the beach, running as fast as she was able to, at six in the morning.

Just her, the water and the seagulls.

One thing down, everything else to go.

Not that there was all that much to get done these days. After handling Alex's and Cris's weddings, she'd discovered she had a real knack for event planning. And while business at the inn was continuing at a steady, brisk pace, there were only a handful of dinner parties for her to put together for the guests. Stevi had suddenly found herself with next to nothing to do.

Without events to plan or classes to study for, she was feeling incredibly restless. It was only a week since graduation, but she was already bored to tears and dying for some sort of excitement.

Stevi accelerated her pace, pushing harder.

Oh, she was well aware that she should be grateful that her life was as good, as comfortable, as it was. There were no deep, dark secrets—or shallow, light ones for that matter—no family rifts. She had a wonderful family, she got along well with her father, her sisters and even her brothers-in-law.

Stevi blew out a breath. She supposed it was some kind of sin in the grand scheme of things to feel this dissatisfied when there wasn't one single bad thing in her life to point a finger at.

But that didn't change the fact that she desperately craved some excitement, something to inspire her art.

That was why, a year ago, she began considering the possibility of moving to New York City, at least for a while. New York City was everything that Ladera was not. It represented a complete change of pace. After all, New York City was the city that never slept.

New York was the home of the incredible Metropolitan Museum of Art. She felt herself growing excited just thinking of the Met.

New York represented the answer to her prayers.

The only thing stopping her from uprooting this second—as impetuous as that sounded, and she was nothing if not admittedly impetuous—was guilt. Stevi knew, even though he hadn't said a word to her, that her father didn't want her to move away, much less move to New York.

Her dad was a warm, loving man. He'd dealt with his share of sorrow and illnesses, but somehow he'd always managed to find a way to get up again after life had given him a devastating punch to the gut. How could she turn her back on a man like that? Her father was a man who thrived on having his family not just close by, but around him.

And so far, they all were.

Granted Alex and Wyatt had a house in Los Angeles, but that was mostly for Wyatt's convenience so he had somewhere to stay when he was in the middle of selling one of his movie scripts. The rest of the time, Wyatt and Alex lived here at the inn.

By choice.

Wyatt had once told her that his fondest memories of his childhood—as well as of his father—were all created here at the inn, where he and Uncle Dan, as she and her sisters all thought of Wyatt's father, spent their summers. And even Cris, who could have lived in a mini-mansion because of Shane's construction skills, stayed at the inn, in the wing Shane had built after he finished the expansion that had brought him here in the first place.

Now Alex and Wyatt were going to have a baby and Cris's five-year-old son, Ricky, was always with his grandfather, so it wasn't as if she'd be abandoning her dad to a life of solitude if she left.

With her younger sister, Andy, rounding out their numbers, there were plenty of family on hand.

Despite that, the thought of leaving the inn made her feel really guilty.

Yet staying here might just drive her stir-crazy.

People came to Ladera-by-the-Sea and willingly paid top dollar to bask in its tranquility, in its soothing peacefulness—in all the things that were driving her away.

Maybe, Stevi tried to console herself, if

she got away for a while, gave New York City an honest try, she might just get it out of her system. Maybe she'd discover that that sort of life really wasn't for her and that what she had right here in her own backyard was what mattered.

But she knew that if she didn't get the opportunity to contrast and compare the two ways of life, she was never really going to appreciate what she had.

Okay, Stevi decided, feeling determined. She had her course of action planned out.

She was going to tell her father that she was going to New York City on an extended vacation, to see the sights and take in the museums and the art galleries. Knowing her father, she was fairly certain he would object if she told him she was undertaking this New York adventure on her own, so she wouldn't mention that part.

Right, and he wouldn't ask who you were going with.

Stevi ran even faster. Her calves protested, threatening to cramp.

Maybe she'd ask one of her friends to come with her. Oh, not for as long as she planned on staying, but just long enough for her to find some temporary place to land. Maybe an apartment being sublet.

Too bad Wyatt no longer lived there, she thought. As a boy, after his parents had gotten divorced, his mother had taken Wyatt to live there.

But then, of course, if he'd never moved out here, he never would have become a screenplay writer, never would have married her sister.

Everything turned out for the best in the end. And it would again.

At least she fervently hoped so.

Her heart rate up, her calves aching, she glanced at her watch to see how long she had been at it.

Stevi frowned as she made out the numbers, then looked up and ahead.

Rather than being on her way back by now, she had just managed to reach the squat sand dune.

That meant she was only halfway finished with her run.

Stevi sighed. There was all that distance to run back. Or walk back if she was too tired, she thought, entertaining the possibility for exactly twenty seconds.

She was in far better shape than that, she reasoned, egging herself on to pick up her pace once again.

"C'mon, Stevi, you can do this. Show your stuff. Run like you mean it, not like some little old lady who can't put one foot in front of the other."

Out of the corner of her eye, she thought she saw something in the distance, something bobbing up and down in the water.

Most likely, she reasoned as she continued running toward it, it was either a dead fish or, as it was nine times out of ten, a large clump of seaweed.

She and her sisters often came down to the beach to clear the seaweed away. Half the time, it smelled like rotten eggs.

She changed direction slightly, running

to where she thought she had spotted the seaweed.

Her eyes widened as she drew closer to the debris that had been washed ashore. Her breath got stuck in her throat.

There was no longer a question in her mind what she was looking at. The clump of seaweed had somehow managed to turn into the very real form of a man.

A man lying very still and facedown in the sand.

She didn't remember how the last fifteen feet were reduced to less than a foot. Couldn't remember if she ran toward the prone body or if she approached it cautiously. Given her usual recklessness, she probably ran.

But suddenly, there she was, standing over the immobile body of a man, wondering if he was dead or just unconscious.

"Mister?" she addressed softly.

There was no indication that he had heard her.

"Mister?" she said a little louder this time.

Still no reaction.

She put her hand on his shoulder and gently shook him. Again, no response.

Was he dead?

So far, in her world, death was something that occurred offstage, like her mother's passing and Uncle Dan's recent demise.

Her breath felt as if it had become solid and was backing up in her throat.

Drawing her courage to her like a shield, Stevi took hold of his shoulder again, rolling him to turn him faceup.

It wasn't easy.

He was far from a small man. She wasn't good at judging things like height, but he had to be well over six feet. And young. Those were sculpted muscles she was pulling on, hard even though they weren't tensed.

When she finally got him on his back so that she could get a better look at him, Stevi's breath caught in her throat.

She had to be looking down into the handsomest face she had ever seen, bar none. And—she was no expert when it came to this—she was fairly sure that was a bullet wound in his chest close to his shoulder.

Now that he was on his back, she saw that he was bleeding.

Tearing the bottom of her oversize T-shirt, she bunched it up into a huge wad and pressed it against the wound. She needed it to stay in place, but it wasn't as though she came equipped with bandages or tape—or rope.

But she had a headband, she thought. Pulling it off, she looped it up his arm to his chest and then tied it as best she could.

Leaning in closer, Stevi tried to find some signs of life, some indication that he was still taking in air and that his heart was beating.

Just when she was inches away from his face, her attention focused on his chest, the man's eyes suddenly flew open.

Stevi stifled a gasp.

"No police," he said in a low, raspy voice, grasping her wrist.

The next second, his hold loosened, his fingers lax against her wrist.

He was unconscious again.

CHAPTER TWO

STEVI STARED DOWN at the man's face. Scores of questions crossed her mind. Questions he couldn't answer because he was unconscious.

Crouching over him, Stevi gingerly placed one hand directly before his nostrils and one on his chest, trying to detect some signs of life. While she didn't feel his heart beating, she did detect just the slightest bit of breath coming from his nose.

She sighed with relief. He was still breathing. But who knew for how long? The makeshift bandage she'd created was discolored from all the blood it was soaking up. She needed to get him up to the inn and from there, to a hospital.

But none of this was going to happen if

she didn't get someone to help her. However, what was she going to say? She didn't know the first thing about this man who had washed up on her beach. Why had someone shot him? Was he some kind of a criminal?

Well, whoever he was, sinner or saint, she couldn't just let him bleed to death.

Her father would know what to do. Rising to her feet, Stevi frowned. Or maybe, since he was stronger, she should get Shane. It was still early and her brother-in-law wouldn't have gone to work yet. He was renovating a house not far from the inn, which meant that he wouldn't be leaving until around seven. People didn't like to hear construction before seven.

The person she really wished she could go to was Wyatt. She'd grown up with him; he was like a big brother to her. Wyatt always knew what to do. But her brother-in-law was in L.A. rewriting one of his scripts.

That wound needed to be treated *now*. Despite what the man had said, the right thing to do was to call the police.... Staring down, she hesitated. Something in her gut—and for the life of her, she wouldn't have been able to say what—told her not to call them. At least, not yet. Not until this man had an opportunity to tell her what had happened.

Until he could speak for himself, she was going to be his voice. And his protector.

She just hoped she wouldn't regret it.

She looked up the hill toward the inn. Was it her imagination, or did it suddenly look to be even farther away than she'd thought?

The winding road that led from the side of the inn down to the beach was just wide enough to accommodate a truck.

Silvio, the inn's gardener, had one.

If she could pull off a last-minute double wedding for her two sisters, she could do anything.

Stevi took off for the inn.

There was an unconscious, bleeding man on the beach depending on her.

"TELL ME AGAIN—and this time I would like to hear the *whole* reason—why do you want my truck?" Silvio Armado Juarez asked his boss's third daughter.

He thought of the girls as his own. He'd found his way to the inn some eighteen years ago, after having been forced to leave Argentina behind. His wife had already taken their three-year-old son and disappeared, and he'd barely managed to scrape enough money together to make it to the United States. He'd already spent most of what was left of his meager savings trying to find them, but never had. And then his time had run out and he'd had to leave. Fast.

The night he'd stumbled into Ladera-by-the-Sea, he certainly wasn't looking for salvation. But in Richard Roman, Silvio wound up finding that and so much more.

Stevi shifted beneath the man's watchful, dark eyes. "I, um, found something on the beach and it's too big for me to carry up."

"You found what on the beach?" It was clear that he wasn't about to budge, or hand over the keys to the truck, until he was satisfied with her answer.

Lying had never been her strong suit. "It's big and clumsy," she explained with a small, careless shrug, praying for the interrogation to be over.

"Everything has a name, Miss Stevi, even big and clumsy things. And if it is that big, then I should put it in the truck for you. Come," he said, putting down the rake, "I will drive us down."

She had no idea how Silvio would react to the man who had washed ashore. She couldn't really even say why she was so determined to keep this whole incident as quiet as possible. Maybe because she'd been the first one on the scene and she felt that this man's fate could very well be in her hands. She didn't want to surrender that responsibility to her father or older sisters or anyone else for that matter.

"No," she insisted forcefully, "really,

I can handle this by myself. I just need your truck."

Silvio looked at her for a long moment. Alexandra was the one who controlled things. Cristina was the one who mothered everyone. Stephanie, this blond-haired young woman with the sparkling blue eyes, was the risk taker, the one who would dive into the ocean without testing the waters first.

"What is it that you are up to, Miss Stevi?" he asked.

"Nothing," she answered far too quickly in his opinion. "I just found something. It might even be gone by now."

For all she knew, the stranger might have come to again and this time, he might have managed to get up and gone—where? There was nowhere for a person in his half-drowned—not to mention shot—condition to go but up here to the inn and in her opinion, the man looked as though he was in no shape to climb the hill.

"Then let us go look together to see if it is gone. If it is not, then we will bring this something you found up to the inn. Agreed?"

The smile Stevi had pasted on her lips took a little more effort to maintain as she realized there was no way around this.

Silvio was coming with her.

She should have known this would happen. Over the years, out of gratitude and allegiance to her father, Silvio had appointed himself their guardian angel-in-chief. Guardian angels, apparently, had tremendous sticking power.

"All right, sure, I could use the extra help," she said.

She followed Silvio to his vehicle, a truck he now owned after paying off his debt to her father over the years. The proud man had insisted on that.

She and Silvio got in the cab. When Silvio placed his hands on the steering wheel, he glanced over toward her, waiting for her to finish buckling up. When she did, he nodded in satisfaction and started up the truck.

As it rumbled to life, Stevi knew she

had precious little time. "Um, Silvio, I'm going to need you to do something for me," Stevi began hesitantly.

"I am listening," he responded, guiding the truck slowly down the winding path.

She pressed her lips together, searching for the right way to phrase this. There really wasn't one. She just had to hope he would grant her this request.

"I would like to keep this a secret between the two of us."

"Keep what a secret between us?" Silvio raised one salt-and-pepper eyebrow.

"It would be just for a little while, until I can get all the facts together," she said, her voice rising as she spoke faster.

"You are not answering my question," Silvio said.

Stevi had never heard him raise his voice. Even so, she and her sisters always knew when the man was less than pleased.

"I need you to agree before I answer you," Stevi blurted out.

While Silvio had come to love all four

of the girls as if they were his daughters, that didn't mean he would allow any of them to lead him blindly. Love, to him, meant giving the other person the benefit of your experience and your honor.

"I cannot agree to something until I know what it is I am agreeing to—and why I am doing something," he said as he kept a watchful eye on the road before him, taking it as slowly as he could. If he went too fast, there was a very real possibility the truck could flip over.

She was running out of time. "Please, Silvio."

"I am not thinking of myself right now," he told Stevi in a very serious voice. "It is you I am worried about."

Ever the guardian angel, she thought. She should have realized that she would be his first concern. She should have set his mind at ease first thing.

"You don't have to be. It's just that you know how excitable my father is and I don't want him needlessly agitated or upset unless there's something to be upset about."

Silvio slowed down even more. There was something up ahead. Less than a beat later, he could make out what it was.

So that was why she was trying to get him to promise his silence.

"Like a strange man lying on the beach?" he asked, sparing her a glance.

"Yes, maybe like that," she admitted, then blinked, taken completely by surprise by his question. "How did you—"

She turned to look through the truck's windshield. The stranger was lying on the beach, exactly the way she'd left him.

"He's still there," she cried.

"Is that your big and clumsy something?"

"Yes." From what she could see, the wounded man hadn't moved a muscle. Did he have any injuries she'd missed? she wondered nervously.

"Who is he?"

This wasn't a time for games, so she told him the truth. "I don't know."

Silvio drew in his breath sharply. "This could be a dangerous man."

He was right, and yet, something inside of her said no. Stevi shook her head. "I don't think so. Please, Silvio, trust me on this."

"It is not you I need to trust," he told her.

Silvio cut his engine when he was less than two feet away from the prone figure. He got out quickly, but not as quickly as she did, as she hurried over to the unconscious man and knelt next to him.

"This man is big," Silvio said. "He is also wounded."

"I know, that's why we need to get him back to the inn before he bleeds out. Maybe if the two of us—"

Silvio waved her words away before she could complete her thought. "You will just get in my way. Open the back of the truck."

As she hurried to do as she was told, Silvio squatted, picked the stranger up and then carried him fireman style.

The only indication Silvio gave that he was struggling beneath the weight was his deep breathing.

"This is against my better judgment," he told Stevi once he had placed his load into the flatbed of his truck.

"I know," Stevi responded and then, impulsively, she kissed Silvio on the cheek.

Silvio looked at her, surprised. "That does not make it all right." Even so, a hint of a smile curved the corners of his mouth.

Stevi nodded. "I know that, too," she replied. "I just wanted to say thank you."

"We need to get back before this man bleeds all over my truck," he said gruffly.

"Absolutely," she agreed with a sigh of relief. She'd made it past the first hurdle.

CHAPTER THREE

AFTER THEIR JOINT wedding in December, and Alex and Cris had moved with their respective husbands into separate wings within the expanded inn, Stevi's room still remained in the main part of the inn, or the "old inn," as her father liked to refer to it. The fastest route to her room, naturally, was through the front entrance.

However, that route would take her, Silvio and the man she'd found on the beach past the reception desk, where Alex could be found most of the day. It would also take them past the kitchen, Cris's second home since she was the inn's resident chef. Stevi opted for another, more roundabout path to get into the inn and, ultimately, to her room.

There were actually several entry points

into the bed-and-breakfast besides the front entrance. There were double French doors at the rear of the inn, frequently used because they led to the wraparound veranda. There were also a couple of single doors located on either side of the inn.

Stevi picked the side door closest to her room.

After parking his truck as closely as he could, Silvio got out of the cab and went straight to the back. The stranger was still unconscious.

"He is losing blood again," Silvio noted, shaking his head. He glanced toward her. "This man should be taken to a hospital."

Silvio wasn't saying anything she wasn't already thinking. "But if we take him to the hospital in this condition, the E.R. physician is going to have to report the wound to the police. Hospital personnel are supposed to report every gunshot wound they treat."

Silvio released the back panel. "It is a good law."

"But we don't know what happened to

him. What if he was trying to save someone and got shot for his trouble?" she asked with feeling. "That makes him a Good Samaritan and since he can't speak for himself, the police are going to assume he's a criminal and handcuff him to the hospital bed until they can get information out of him. You wouldn't want a hero to be treated like a common criminal, would you?"

Silvio remained unconvinced. "You do not know he is a hero."

Stevi was quick to take the other side. "You don't know that he's not."

Silvio sighed wearily. "You are making my head hurt, Miss Stevi. Does your father ever complain about arguing with you?"

She grinned. "All the time. C'mon, we have to get him into my room before anyone sees him and starts asking questions I can't answer yet."

The gardener looked at her dubiously even as he picked up the unconscious man and once again positioned him over his shoulder.

"As in why are you doing this?" he asked, grunting slightly under the full weight of the unconscious man.

"Something like that," she answered.

Silvio murmured a few words under his breath in Spanish as Stevi led the way. Entering the inn through the side door, they took the less-traveled, roundabout and longer route to her room.

Stevi felt as if she held her breath the entire way. When they finally reached her room without running into anyone from her family, or any of the inn's guests, she felt almost giddy.

She immediately shut the door behind Silvio and finally let go of the breath she'd been holding.

"Made it," she declared triumphantly in a whisper.

"Yes," Silvio agreed, laying his burden on her bed as best he could. "But what is it that you have made?"

The way Silvio posed it made it sound

like a philosophical question. She shrugged. "I guess we'll find out, won't we?" she said, half to herself. She frowned as she took a closer look at the bedraggled stranger's chest. "We're going to have to do something about that wound." She tried to remember what she had learned in a basic first-aid class she'd impulsively taken because a guy she'd had a crush on had taken it. Nothing had come of the would-be relationship and right now she couldn't recall anything useful from the class, either.

"Bring me some gauze, some rubbing alcohol and a needle and thread," Silvio instructed in a no-nonsense voice.

That sounded like something a person with medical training would request. She had never known Silvio as anything other than a gardener.

"Silvio?" She looked at him, puzzled.

"He is bleeding again. That wound must be cleaned and closed up." There was no emotion in his voice, just a pure statement of fact.

Could you close up a wound if there

was a bullet lodged in the body? "But the bullet—"

"Has gone straight through and it looks as if it missed everything important," he answered. "I saw that when I picked him up. That is also why he is bleeding so much. There is nothing to get in the way of the blood leaving his body. Hurry."

Getting rubbing alcohol and gauze was not a problem. Each of the inn's bathrooms, including her own, came equipped with those items.

The needle and thread were trickier, until she remembered that Dorothy, the head housekeeper, took it upon herself to mend the simple tears of the guests' clothing.

Having had the occasion to look into Dorothy's rather large sewing basket when the housekeeper had brought it out once, she knew the woman had a wide variety of threads and a full selection of sewing needles to choose from.

She also knew that Dorothy didn't bother locking her door. It reflected on the kind of atmosphere that the inn prided itself on. Here everyone was treated like a trusted family member.

Knocking first to make sure she wouldn't be walking in on Dorothy, Stevi gave the housekeeper to the count of twenty before opening the door. That's when Stevi remembered that the housekeeper had gone for a much-needed rest to visit with friends in Ohio. Stevi slipped in, then quickly closed the door behind her.

Dorothy's small room would have made a nun's quarters look almost frivolous. The only visible item that was in the least bit personal was a framed photograph that had been taken a couple of Christmases ago in the reception area by one of the guests. Dorothy and the entire Roman family, including Cris's son, Ricky, were standing in front of a ten-foot Christmas tree.

The sewing box she was looking for was next to the only upholstered chair in the room. Both faced the window for better light, she guessed.

Opening the sewing box quickly, Stevi picked up a spool of white thread and a needle that looked to be of average thickness and length. Pausing, she wondered if Silvio would rather use a thinner needle. Or a thicker one? Unable to decide, she took three and hoped she wasn't missing something obvious.

She quickly closed the sewing box, leaving it where she found it.

She opened the door just a crack to make sure no one was passing by. Most people were either still in their rooms or had gone to the dining area for breakfast, which meant she was relatively safe, she reasoned, as she slipped out of Dorothy's room and hurried back to her own.

"Got it," she declared, leaning against the door she'd just closed, looking for all the world like a fugitive who had outrun her pursuer.

"Did you have to drive into town to get it?" Silvio asked. His eyes remained on the unconscious patient as he held out his hand to her.

"It wasn't easy to find," she answered defensively. Coming forward, she placed the spool of thread in his hand. When he looked at her quizzically, she produced the three needles. He took the midsize one.

Silvio had already used the alcohol and gauze to wash the area around the wound and to try to stem the flow of blood.

As she watched, he measured out a length of thread, snapped it away from the spool and threaded the needle after first dousing it with alcohol.

Then, with a sure hand, he methodically sewed up the man's wound. With each stitch he took, he spared a glance toward the unconscious man's face, waiting for some sort of reaction or sign that he was waking up. But the man continued to be unconscious.

Mercifully, Stevi thought, the stranger wasn't awake to feel the needle.

Finished with his handiwork, Silvio bit the end of his thread.

The stitches were small, neat and parallel. Gardeners, she was certain, didn't know how to sew like that. Most people didn't sew like that.

She looked at the man she had known almost from the very beginning of her life. What he had just demonstrated took training.

"Silvio?" she said uncertainly.

"Yes?" he responded, a guarded note in his voice.

"Where did you learn to sew like that?"

He shrugged. "I had a mother who was too busy to take care of the seven children she had given birth to, so I did what I could to help out."

Stevi frowned. The stitches were more professional than those of a child who was desperate.

"And you sewed their clothes?" she asked, trying to coax more out of him.

"Sometimes," he said with another shrug. "I also might have learned how to do that while I worked at the hospital."

She really hadn't known what sort of work Silvio had done in a hospital in his past. She'd made a few assumptions, she now realized. This was not the skill set of an orderly or a janitor.

Just who was this man her father had taken in all those years ago?

"Silvio?" she pressed.

"Yes?" His back was to her as he tried to make his patient as comfortable as possible.

Placing his fingers against the man's pulse, he silently counted the beats, then quadrupled them. The heart rate was getting stronger, he thought with satisfaction. He hoped that this—caring for the stranger—didn't turn out to be a mistake on his part.

He empathized with this stranger. In a manner of speaking, all those years ago he had been the one who had washed up on the shore. His shore had happened to be Richard Roman.

"What did you do at the hospital?"

Her question made Silvio lift his head as he stopped what he was doing. For a second, he stared straight ahead without turning to face her.

He decided a partial answer might be enough, so he told her quietly over his shoulder, "I was a physician's aide."

For a moment, she forgot all about the man lying in her bed and looked instead at the man she considered part of her family.

"Then what are you doing here?" He had a vocation, an ability to help people heal. Why would he be satisfied gardening?

Silvio turned around, his face the picture of earnestness. "Tending to your mother's garden because your father asked me to."

Stevi still had trouble accepting and processing the information. "Don't you miss being a physician's aide?"

There was a calmness in his voice as he answered her question. "If I missed it, Miss Stevi, I would be there. Instead, I am here, helping your father. Helping you," he added, looking from her to the man he'd helped bring into her room.

It took all kinds to make a world, she

reminded herself. And she didn't want Silvio to think that she was questioning his judgment.

"I guess things work themselves out for the best."

As to that, Silvio wasn't 100 percent convinced, at least, not in this particular case. "That still remains to be seen, Miss Stevi."

The patient appeared to be breathing more easily now, she thought. And it might have been her imagination, but she thought his color was a little better. A little less pale at any rate.

"How long do you think he'll be unconscious?" she asked.

"That is difficult to say," Silvio said. "The man has lost a lot of blood, but that appears to be the only wound. Since you do not want to take him to a hospital—"

"I don't," she said with feeling. "At least not until he can speak for himself."

The expression on Silvio's face was stern. "Hopefully, it will not be too late by then."

"It won't be," she answered.

"How can you be so sure?" It wasn't a challenge so much as a desire to know why she was so confident she was right.

"I just am," she answered.

Silvio sighed. He was going to have to step up his efforts to watch over this family. "Then we will just have to wait and see," he said calmly, like a man who was going to sit back and wait for things to unfold.

He rose from the side of the bed. From his perspective, there was nothing else he could do until the man woke up. But there was just one more thing he needed to know.

"When will you tell your father about this?" he pressed.

She nodded toward the stranger. "Not until he wakes up and can tell me what happened to him."

She saw the doubt on Silvio's face. She knew he was worried about her and she appreciated that the man cared enough to concern himself this way about her—

about her whole family, really. But from her point of view, she was being rational in her decision.

"I need to have something more to tell my father than 'Look what I found on the beach today, Dad. It washed up on the shore right at my feet. Can I keep it?' I want to be able to explain how he came to be here and why he has that bullet wound in his chest. Or Dad will think I'm crazy."

Silvio's eyes locked onto hers. "I could see your father's point."

"I know, I know," Stevi agreed.

She closed her eyes as she searched her mind for something she could say that would ease Silvio's doubts.

"On some level, so can I," she finally admitted. "And I really can't explain why, but something tells me that bringing him here, having you take care of him, instead of carting him off to the nearest hospital and handing him off to be someone else's problem, is the right thing to do."

He appeared unconvinced. "Right for who, Miss Stevi? Him? Or you?"

Again, she didn't have anything logical to offer as an explanation. A gut feeling didn't really translate all that well into logic.

"Maybe both. Him, definitely."

"And if he is a criminal?" Silvio pressed.

But he's not. I just know it. She flashed the gardener a smile. "Then you and Shane and Wyatt will protect me."

"And who will protect me from your father when he finds out that I let you do this?"

Stevi's grin grew wider, brighter, as she answered, "Why, me, of course."

Silvio shook his head. There was no amusement in his eyes.

"You will forgive me, Miss Stevi," he told her solemnly, "but I do not find your assurance to be comforting. I do not like lying to the man who took me in without question."

"Did you ever think that my father might want to do the same thing for this man?" she challenged.

Try as she might, she couldn't read Silvio's expression or guess what he was thinking.

"If you feel that way, then why are you hiding him in your room?" Silvio posed. "Why do we not go to your father right now and tell him?"

Silvio responded only to the truth, so she gave him an honest answer. "Because he asked me to help him and right now, this is part of it."

Silvio looked at her in surprise. "He talked to you?"

She nodded.

Silvio frowned and sighed mightily. "I do not know where to begin. Do you know what kind of a chance you took?" he asked. "When you saw him lying on the beach like that, you should have come to get me right away. This man could have hurt you."

"He was half-drowned and he had a bullet wound in his chest. This man couldn't have hurt a sand flea," she protested, waving a hand.

"He could have been pretending to be

unconscious so that he could overpower you," Silvio pointed out.

She laughed.

"The beach was deserted. How could he have even known I was coming?" She looked at him and knew her words were falling on deaf ears. "You're going to go on worrying about this, aren't you?"

He didn't answer her directly. "We will have this conversation again *after* you tell your father."

She nodded her agreement. "Okay, it's a deal." Silvio crossed back to the door. She saw the hesitation in his eyes as he looked back over his shoulder at the man on her bed.

"I do not like leaving you with him."

"He's wounded," she reminded him. "Not to mention unconscious."

Silvio still didn't budge. "What will you do?" he asked.

She wasn't sure what he was really asking, so she told him exactly what she intended to do next. "Take a shower, change, get some breakfast. The usual."

The frown on his square, tanned face deepened. "You are going to undress?"

She answered his question as seriously as she could. "I find taking a shower with my clothes on doesn't get me as clean as I'd like."

He didn't crack a smile. "Lock the bathroom door."

CHAPTER FOUR

SMILING TO HERSELF, she flipped the lock on her bedroom door as a precautionary measure. Not because she didn't want Silvio to walk in—he was the only one she actually didn't mind coming in at this point. However, if anyone else walked in and saw the stranger in bed while she was in the shower, she would have to do a great deal of explaining really quickly.

"Silvio doesn't trust you," she said to the stranger lying on top of her comforter— she was probably going to have to get a new one, she realized. Blood didn't always wash out. "Are you trustworthy?" she asked as she stood studying his face. It was a handsome face, but did it belong to a man who was ultimately trustworthy? A man who told the truth at all times, not just when it was convenient? "Am I being a fool to think I'm safe with you? How did you get on our beach?" she wondered out loud. "And who shot you and why? Or was this just an unfortunate accident?

"Boy, I can't wait until you regain consciousness. I've got so many questions for you. Questions you're going to have to answer truthfully or I'm going to be so disappointed in you," she said. "I'm climbing out on this limb and it's not very comfortable out here to say the least."

She straightened.

"I'd better get into that shower or I'm never going to leave this room." With that, she grabbed the clothes she intended to wear that day—a pair of denim shorts and a blue tank top—and hurried into the bathroom. She remembered to lock that door before she stepped into the shower.

THE WOMAN'S VOICE came to him from a great, long distance. It sounded melodic. It also sounded fast. So fast he could only vaguely make out what she was saying.

Something about trust and not lying, he thought. Or maybe he was wrong. Maybe it was about something else.

It didn't matter.

He was probably dreaming. He'd been winking in and out for a while now.

Splintered memories began coming to him in fragmented bits and pieces. The last thing he remembered was pain exploding in his chest and someone throwing him overboard—or had he jumped?—while someone else was cursing that he should have been tied up first, just in case.

He remembered trying to swim, trying to find where the shore was. Remembered telling himself not to panic, that if he panicked, then he was lost.

Dead.

Was he dead?

He'd never believed all that much, not like his mother, but now he would have liked to believe that there was something after life was finally over. Some kind of continuation.

Man but he was tired.

So tired.

He needed to rest, needed to get away from this burning in his shoulder.

Rest.

Was that it? Was this eternal rest, forever and peaceful?

He was too tired to think. He'd think about that later, when he wasn't too tired anymore....

Provided there was a later....

STEVI HURRIED OUT of the bathroom freshly dressed, her hair still wet. Her footprints marking her passage from the bathroom into her bedroom were slightly damp as well, leaving an impression first on the floor and then on the rug.

She took no notice. Her attention was on the man in bed.

"Still not with us, huh?" she observed. Was there someone searching for him this very moment, or was he a loner, the answer to her prayer for some excitement?

Right, special delivery.

Taking a hairbrush from her bureau, she brushed her hair back, out of the way. When it dried, it would be curlier than usual, but she really didn't care about that right now. She had a job to do.

"Well, maybe you need all that extra sleep to get over what you've been through. We'll talk about that later, too. Right now, I'm going to get some breakfast. Don't worry," she quickly interjected as if he had actually rendered an opinion. "I'll bring some back for you." She cocked her head, like someone trying to make out a low voice. "Which would you like, pancakes or eggs?" She nodded, coming to her own conclusion. "Okay, I'll bring you both, no sense in starving you, right? I won't be long," she promised.

With that, Stevi left her room and eased her door closed, then locked it so that no one would enter while she was gone. When she turned to hurry down the hallway, she walked smack into her younger sister.

Andy glanced at the closed door. "Who

are you talking to?" she asked without preamble.

Startled, Stevi slipped her arm through Andy's and headed for the dining room as if this had already been prearranged. "Excuse me?"

"I said who are you talking to?" Andy repeated, just as she found it a wee bit strange that Stevi was almost pulling her toward the dining room. "I could hear you through the door when I walked by just now."

"Myself, I was talking to myself," Stevi told her cheerfully.

"Really?" Andy looked at her. "Because you were talking in full sentences and it sounded as if you were asking what you wanted for breakfast."

"I was," Stevi replied without hesitation. "I can't decide between pancakes and scrambled eggs this morning. I always talk to myself," she added, as if it was the most natural thing.

Andy frowned. "Since when?" She wanted to know.

"Since forever," Stevi answered in the same cheerful voice. "Nobody else listens to me so I might as well talk to myself, right? You probably do it, too. You just haven't realized it."

"No, I don't and if I did, I would have realized it," Andy protested. Stevi opened her mouth again, but Andy held up her hand to stop the flow of words. "So what did you decide?"

"About what?" Stevi asked cautiously. Was Andy playing her? Had Andy caught a glimpse of the sleeping mystery man?

"Eggs or pancakes?" Andy prompted. "You know, your big breakfast debate."

"Oh, that," she said, sighing with relief. "Both, actually."

"Both?" Andy echoed as they walked into the dining area. "Stevi, you hardly ever finish a meal. Just how do you think you're going to manage to put away two?"

"Don't worry about it—I feel hungry," she said, avoiding looking at her. "This is the new me, no longer obsessed with getting the best grades, worrying if I'd gained half a pound. You have no idea what a relief it is not to have to study anymore." That, at least, was true. She'd lived with that pressure for a long time and it was finally over. It could also explain why she felt somewhat at loose ends. Happy, but restless. "I feel like a new woman. A free woman."

"So what's the free woman going to be doing with all her free time? Besides jogging on the beach at ungodly hours, I mean," Alex said, coming up behind the two of them.

"I'm still trying to figure that out," Stevi answered.

"Well, here's something for you to think about while you're doing that figuring. You really are a good event planner." Alex picked a table for the three of them and sat down. Andy slid in on her right, but Stevi remained standing. "The inn could use that talent of yours, you know."

She never had any doubts that the inn would always be her fallback plan, somewhere she could turn to if things fell apart. But she didn't want to settle; she wanted something to be passionate about, like Cris with her cooking, or Alex with running the inn.

"And Dad would be tickled pink if you decided to stay on at the inn," Alex added.

"Dad doesn't look good in pink," Stevi deadpanned.

Although she knew her father wanted all of them to have ambitions, to follow their dreams, she also knew that her father was hopeful that all their dreams could be fulfilled within a ten-mile radius—if not closer.

"You know what I mean." Then, before Stevi had a chance to say anything in response, Alex warned, "Don't argue with a pregnant woman. It's not safe."

Still standing over her sister, Stevi grinned. "For whom? Me or the pregnant woman?"

"Why, you, of course," Alex retorted. "Why aren't you sitting down, Stevi? It's hurting my neck, having to look up to talk to you."

Stevi made no effort to take a seat. Instead, her smile grew. "Now you know how we feel around you all the time." Alex had always been taller than the rest of them. "Why don't you two tell me what you want for breakfast and I'll go in and give your orders to Cris."

Andy looked at her in surprise. "You're playing waitress now?"

Stevi turned in her direction. "I'm playing the good sister," she said, correcting her younger sibling. "Take advantage while you can."

"Does that mean you're going to be leaving for New York, after all?"

Although 85 percent certain that a stay in New York was in her near future, she wasn't committed to it yet—at least, not the admitting part of the process yet. She had a few things to work out, not the least of which was coming up with an acceptable way to tell her father.

"No, that means I'm liable to decide not to be the good sister and let you two fend for yourselves. Until then, orders, please?" she pressed, looking from Alex to Andy.

Because Alex was still undecided, Stevi took Andy's order first. Bacon, toast and coffee.

"I'm ready now," Alex said a second later. Unlike Andy, Alex's order went on for two minutes and included practically everything on the breakfast menu.

Amused, Stevi grinned at her older sister. "You do realize you're just eating for two, not an entire regiment, right?"

Alex frowned. Her hormones all over the map these days, Alex didn't appreciate criticism of her eating habits. "I'm eating for two but throwing up for one so I need to order for three," she said.

Stevi heard the edge in her sister's voice. Alex hadn't exactly ever been the easiest person to get along with, not anywhere nearly as easygoing as Cris. But this was more irate than normal.

"You planning on being like this the entire pregnancy?" She wanted to know.

"Yes," Alex said with finality. "And beyond, as well. I find I like ordering people around."

"You always did," Stevi replied with a dramatic sigh. She glanced at the notes she'd just made on the palm of her hand. "Let me see if there's enough food in the kitchen for this." She quickly ducked through the swinging door into the kitchen before Alex had a chance to fire back.

CHAPTER FIVE

"ALEX WILL TAKE one refrigerator, to go," Stevi announced as she walked into the kitchen. Her sister had her back to her and was busy preparing an order on the industrial stove. "Seriously, Alex thinks she's eating for a small village and wants, like, one of practically everything on the breakfast menu. And Andy will have her usual two slices of warm bread, a cup of albino, supersweet coffee and three slices of burnt bacon."

"And you?" Cris asked, glancing up from the omelet she was preparing for one of the guests.

"The run made me kind of hungry this morning. Could you fix me an order of pancakes and some scrambled eggs with ham?" she asked.

Ordinarily, she ate a light breakfast, sometimes even leaving half on her plate. She slanted a glance toward Cris, hoping her request wouldn't set off any alarms.

The change didn't go unnoticed. "Wow, that is a lot for you," Cris commented.

Stevi shrugged. "Yes, I know. Must be all that great sea air."

"The air's been there all along, Stevi," Cris pointed out.

"I've got it, boss," Jorge, Cris's chief assistant, called out. He nodded toward Stevi.

"Thanks." Cris flashed him a grateful, weary smile.

"No problem," Jorge responded. "You just take it easy, boss. You're working too hard, as usual."

So preoccupied with getting back to her bedroom as quickly as possible, Stevi hadn't really been paying attention to much else. But Jorge's comment about Cris working too hard made her take a closer look at Cris. It occurred to her that her older sister was looking rather pale.

She automatically reached out to put her hand against Cris's forehead. Cris pulled her head back.

"What are you doing?"

"Just wanted to see if you had a fever," Stevi explained, dropping her hand. "You look a little peaked."

"No fever," Cris answered dismissively.

It wasn't like Cris to be so curt. Something was up, Stevi thought. "You coming down with something?"

Cris laughed softly. "No, I'm fine."

Now her curiosity was fully aroused. "Don't lie to the woman who pulled a rabbit out of the hat and piggybacked a real wedding for you on to Alex's when you realized how much you'd missed, practically eloping on the run. You owe me."

She was practically daring Cris to argue the point. No one ever won an argument with her, unless, occasionally, it was Alex.

"I'm not lying," Cris protested. "I'm not coming down with anything, not in the traditional sense."

Stevi's curiosity went up another notch.

"Okay, how about in the nontraditional sense?" Stevi pressed. Interrupting herself for a second, she looked toward Jorge and made a request. "Could you make that to go, please, Jorge?"

Jorge nodded.

"You're taking breakfast to go?" Cris asked. "What's the matter, you suddenly don't like my dining room?"

"It's not that," she protested, noting that somehow, Cris's domain had spread from the kitchen to the dining area, as well. "I've got a few things to do in my room, wise guy, so I thought I'd eat and work at the same time. And don't think you're changing the subject that easily."

"There is no subject to change," Cris said, turning back to flip the omelet.

Stevi shifted so that she was able to at least see Cris's profile. "We have a slight difference of opinion there."

"I'm fine," Cris insisted once again. "Just a little woozy, maybe."

If Cris admitted to being dizzy, then there was more she wasn't saying.

"Cris, Jorge can take over. Heck, even I can do some cooking in an emergency—"

"The emergency would be *after* you started cooking," Cris interjected.

Stevi ignored the comment. "There's no shame if you take a sick day once in a while. Nobody expects you to be invincible. If you caught a bug, then—"

"It's not a bug," Cris protested, losing her patience. "It's a baby."

Stevi's jaw dropped open. "Whoa. Back up. You caught a *baby?*"

Cris sighed. "It wasn't supposed to come out like this.... But it was bound to come out sometime. Yes, in a manner of speaking, I guess."

Stevi's eyes widened even more. "Then you're—"

Closing her eyes, Cris nodded. "Yes, I am," she said.

Jorge was grinning ear to ear. "Congratulations, boss."

Cris inclined her head, uttering a modest, "Thank you."

The surge of pure joy was a beat late,

but when it came, it all but exploded within her. "Cris, why didn't you *say* anything?" Stevi threw her arms around her sister, hugging her hard. "That's wonderful! Why are you keeping it such a secret?" Granted Cris was one of the more quiet of the Roman daughters, but when she discovered she was pregnant with Ricky, everyone in the family knew within about twenty-four hours.

"I didn't want to steal any of Alex's thunder," she confided. "I've already had one baby. This is Alex's first."

That was not a valid reason as far as Stevi was concerned. "Alex can deal with sharing the spotlight, she's not a narcissist. And it's not like you could've kept this a secret forever, you know. Eventually, we would have figured it out. So, does anyone else know?"

Cris inclined her head. "Shane."

"Well, of course! What about Ricky?"

"I would have loved to have included him in this, but if he knew, then the immediate world would have known, as well."

Stevi laughed in agreement.

"There's no such thing as keeping a secret as far as my boy is concerned—especially if it was labeled a secret. The information would have burst out of him the very first opportunity he had. Prefaced with 'Mommy doesn't want anyone to know, but—'"

"Well, always a good thing to let the father know anyway," Stevi said, patting Cris's hand.

"Your breakfast, Miss Stevi," Jorge said, placing a large brown bag on the steel counter next to her.

"Thank you." She flashed the assistant a quick smile.

"Please don't tell everyone," Cris begged her.

"Of course not! I think that kind of information should come from you." She rolled her eyes. "But make sure you call Dad in and tell him first. He'll appreciate being told before the others."

Cris smiled as she placed her hand on her still very flat stomach. "I guess you're right—for a change."

That was the nature of their relationship. Nothing serious could be left alone for long. There was always a bite of sarcasm, a zinger attached somewhere. The Roman sisters were determined not to get mushy on one another.

"Can you get Dad for me, Stevi?" Cris requested. "Ask him to come to the dining area?"

Any other time…but she was acutely aware of the time and she had left her mystery man alone in her room for far too long. What if he had awakened while she was gone? What if he had wandered off? She couldn't have that. Not until she got their stories straight. Otherwise, she would be on the receiving end of a lifetime of lectures from not just her father, but everyone else in the family, as well.

"I'd really love to, Cris, but there's something important I have to get to." She looked at Jorge. "Jorge, can you get my father down here, please? There," she told Cris. "All done. Gotta fly." She grabbed the large brown bag Jorge had brought her and left the kitchen through the back delivery entrance.

She left a bemused Cris staring after her in her wake.

Stevi circumvented the veranda at the back of the inn and made her way to the same side entrance she and Silvio had used earlier. Again, this was the long way around but if she'd gone out through the dining area, Alex and Andy would have grilled her.

The way she saw it, it was better to avoid questions altogether until she had some viable answers.

As she skirted the grounds, her thoughts went back to what she'd just discovered. Cris was going to have another baby. That made two babies being born in the not-too-distant future. Life was moving right along for Alex and Cris, she thought with a touch of envy. They each had a great husband and now they were busy creating their own families.

And where did that leave her?

Confused and restless, that's where, she thought.

Not just that, but with an unidentified man lying in her bed, unconscious to boot.

Life had certainly gone from dull to extremely tangled in a few short hours, Stevi thought as she reached her door.

It was still closed, she noted. Either the stranger was still inside—or he had made an orderly escape, closing the door behind him after he departed.

Holding her breath, Stevi tested it: still locked. Turning the key, she eased the door open.

Her mystery man was just where she had left him, sleeping in bed. Coming a step closer, she never took her eyes off the man. Just as on the beach, he didn't look as if he'd even moved a muscle since she had left.

She set the bag of food down on the

writing desk in the corner, then quietly crept over to the bed.

She studied the man for a long moment. "Are you getting better, or worse?" she wondered out loud. "Am I helping you by keeping you hidden here, or am I destroying any chance you might have to get well? I wish I had a little guidance here," she admitted. "There's nothing on the internet to cover this situation. Can't type in 'What to do with an unknown, unconscious man encountered on the beach' and have Ask.com come up with an answer."

She had hoped that he might be up by now and able to eat, at least a little. He needed to build up his strength after all that blood he lost. When she'd picked up the two orders, she'd wanted to give him first choice of breakfast.

But since it appeared he was going to be out for a while, she decided to eat one and leave the other covered plate for him.

Choosing the eggs and ham, she brought the plate to his bed and sat in the chair she'd pulled over earlier. She took a bite absently and her taste buds almost sprang to life. She'd forgotten that it was impossible to eat anything that Cris prepared absently. It was a gift, she decided.

"You're missing a really good breakfast," she told her sleeping mystery man. "But, knowing Cris, she'd be happy to whip up another order if you like scrambled eggs." Her words came back to her and Stevi laughed shortly. "Here I am, second-guessing what you like to eat and I don't even know your name, or who you are, or what you're actually doing here on our beach."

There had been no wallet, no driver's license, no ID of any kind on his person. Silvio had gone through his pockets the moment he had the man on the bed. It had made Silvio more suspicious.

"So who are you?" Stevi asked. "What do I call you? Are you with some drug cartel and you got caught in the middle of something really bad? Bad enough to bring out guns?

"Or are you some wealthy playboy

whose cabin cruiser got boarded by pirates? Right...there aren't any pirates trolling the coast of Southern California," she reminded herself. "You know, I'm really running out of guesses here. You'd better come to soon and help me out or Silvio will insist that we call the hospital and they'll take one look at you and call the police...and I have this gut feeling that won't be a good thing to do. Am I right?"

He went on sleeping.

Finished with breakfast—which she had wolfed down in between questions—she set the plate aside on her writing desk. Leaning forward, she pushed aside a lock of medium brown hair that had fallen over his eyes.

"Who are you?" Stevi whispered. "Are you ever going to wake up and tell me?"

She supposed the real question here should be, was he ever going to wake up, period? What if he had slipped into an actual coma? She didn't know much about things like that but she'd heard that those kinds of conditions could go on indefinitely.

Maybe forever.

Then what?

Then she'd tell her father everything and ask for his help. Get professional medical care.

She knew that even though Richard Roman might get annoyed with her for having done something that she was certain he would label "dangerous and foolish," he wouldn't waste time with recriminations. He'd just handle it, the way he handled everything else that came his way.

To her, her father was one of the dependable forces of nature. A great comfort to her.

But for the time being, Stevi needed to prove herself—not in anyone else's eyes but her own.

She looked up to her two older sisters, Alex and Cris. Their lives were basically set, their paths more or less chosen and mapped out, while hers felt as if it was scattered all over the place and right smack in the middle of it was this slanted incline, perfect for skateboarding. And right now, she was going down it, ninety-seven miles an hour.

Could she execute the move, or was she going to crash and burn?

She had no idea.

"You're going to have to hurry up, you know," she told him. "I can only hold everyone off for so long. Right now, I can tell them that I'm working on a painting and that I don't want to be disturbed. They'll buy that. The family's usually pretty good about that sort of thing," she confided. "They give me my space, which in this case is actually *your* space. But sometime or other, they're going to want to see a painting, so pull your act together and come around. In the next twenty-four hours, please." Then she added, "Even faster would be nice."

Boy, that had to have sounded weird to him if he could hear her.

"I don't mean to rush you but hiding

you in my room and not telling Dad or any of them about this is making things difficult for me. I'm not much on keeping secrets, if you must know, so the sooner you can open those eyes of yours, the better it'll be for both of us."

Picking up the coffee Jorge had slipped in the bag, she took off the lid. She sat sipping and staring thoughtfully at the unconscious man.

Her brain was going in three directions at once, all at top speed, coming up with different theories, each more fantastic than the last.

"Maybe you're a spy. Or a secret agent." Her words echoed back in her head and she stared at him even more intently, as if that would give her some sort of an answer. "Omigod, could I be sent to prison for harboring you? Worse, could my family get into trouble for this?" The thought of getting her family into trouble over something she was doing horrified her. "Maybe I'd better call the police," she said, automatically reaching for the phone that was on the nightstand by her bed.

But then she stopped midreach. That same gut told her the details about this situation would eventually be brought to light and that she wouldn't be found guilty of doing anything except saving a man from bleeding to death.

Maybe a man who mattered in the corporate world. Or the political arena. Someone important.

"Are you someone important?" she whispered, staring at him. He didn't look familiar to her, but then, that didn't mean anything. She wasn't exactly up on news other than the headlines.

Stevi sighed, frustrated and helpless. She was the type who read the end of a mystery thriller before she invested herself in reading it at all. This situation was already dragging on too long for her liking.

You wanted an adventure, something to happen out of the ordinary, something exciting. Remember?

She pressed her lips together. *Careful what you wish for, right?*

He didn't stir.

"Just hurry up and come to, okay?" And then she laughed to herself. "I've heard about the strong, silent type, but this is really raising the bar pretty high."

She grinned then drained the remainder of her coffee and set the cup down again. "I bet they called you gabby at school."

The man made no answer.

HE WAS HEARING it again, hearing that voice, that soft female voice whispering through his mind, teasing his subconscious as he tried to place it, tried to remember if he'd ever heard it before.

The words she was saying were becoming more distinct, more audible. He could almost make them out.

Almost.

But they still seemed garbled.

Try as he might, he couldn't fight his

way to the surface either, up above this oppressive hazy cloud that enshrouded him and was keeping him down.

CHAPTER SIX

THERE WAS A LIGHT, just a glimmer of it, really, winking in and out along the water far above his head. At first, it seemed to be more than an infinity away.

Unreachable.

But he knew that if he could just hold on long enough to break through the surface, then he could get some air for his all but bursting lungs.

He'd be all right then. He'd be all right.

It was miles and miles away, but he couldn't give up. Couldn't. He had to reach it. Giving up was for losers and he wasn't a loser.

Given a losing hand at birth, he'd still found a way not to lose.

Hadn't he proven that already? Beating the odds, surviving the bad neighborhoods, the indifferent families who gave him a bed to sleep in but were only in it for the money?

He was nobody's kid.

Just a kid.

But he didn't let it break him, didn't let it drag him down. He'd hung on, struggled, *made* something of himself. Made a difference.

Where was it? Where was the surface? It had to be here somewhere.

With his very last ounce of strength, he finally broke through, finally made it to the top of the water.

Air, sweet, wonderful air.

He gulped it in, trying to get enough. Trying to make up for the numbing lack of it.

His temples were pounding, his body aching something fierce. And there was this all-engulfing pain—more like a fire— that had taken over his left side.

Orientation followed.

He remembered.

Remembered what had happened, remembered *why* he'd almost succumbed to the watery grave.

Spinning around, he searched for the cabin cruiser. Instead of right beside him, it was now some distance away.

Heading away from him.

No matter, getting back on it wasn't exactly a viable option. He was outnumbered, outgunned. The only way it would work for him—for his survival—was if he managed to get the drop on all of them and in his present condition, that wasn't a possibility.

He had one chance, only one. He had to swim for shore.

But which way was it?

Slowly turning, moving in a circle, he searched for the vaguest signs of land. There had to be something.

Something.

He thought he heard seagulls and searched for them even though he knew they could just as easily be heading for the open water as they could for land. He searched anyway.

There was nothing else to cling to.

And then he saw them. Saw two seagulls descending in the distance.

Disappearing in the distance.

He might as well die swimming toward the promise of *something* than die out here, treading water. Going nowhere.

Pain knifed through him with every stroke he took, and his left arm held him back. To compensate, he poured it on with his right.

The more he swam, the farther away the shore appeared. It couldn't be moving. And yet, it was.

He wasn't going to make it. He was going to die out here.

Die and nobody would even know what happened to him. That he had been on the right side.

No, it was too soon for him to die.

Too soon!

GULPING AIR, HE realized that his eyes were shut and he forced them open as he sucked in more air, gasping as it went in.

He tried to get up but hands restrained him. Gentle hands. But stronger than he was right now.

Where…? He was in the middle of the ocean.

Wasn't he?

The fire scissored through his chest, cutting it to ribbons.

"It's okay. You're safe now," a woman told him in a soft voice.

He'd heard her voice before. But that had been a hallucination, hadn't it? Was he hallucinating now? Or could this actually be real? The pressure of her hands had felt real.

His eyes had closed again and he pried them opened. There she was, still standing over him. She had to be real. A honey-blonde vision trying to restrain him.

"Who—who are you?"

Was that his voice? It couldn't be. It sounded so weak, so raspy. And yet, it really hurt to talk. Each word felt like a shard of glass being scraped along his throat.

Stevi hovered over the stranger, worried that he might try to get up again. He was clearly weak and more than likely, his legs wouldn't hold him.

"I'm the woman who found you on the beach and brought you back to the inn," she told him.

The man's expression was blank as he repeated, "The inn?"

"My inn," Stevi told him. Convinced he was going to stay put, she released her hold on him and sank into the chair beside the bed. "Well, actually, it's my family's inn, but we all own a piece of it. My dad wanted it that way." That part probably made no difference to this man. She had to remember to stop volunteering more information than people wanted. "What happened to you?"

Wait a minute, he thought. If this woman wasn't a hallucination, if he'd been pulled back into the cruiser and she was working for the people who had tried to kill him, then he couldn't admit to anything. He couldn't break now. There'd been accusations, coupled with torture, but he hadn't admitted a thing, hadn't said a word to save himself and end the torture.

"I don't know," he finally managed to get out.

Stevi sat back in her chair, staring at him incredulously. "You don't know," she repeated. "You don't know who shot you?"

Crenshaw. Larry Crenshaw shot me.

Or at least Crenshaw was responsible for the bullet that had been fired at him. Even if the man hadn't pulled the trigger.

If he hadn't jerked away, the bullet could have easily found his heart—and ended everything.

It started coming back to him.

He hadn't been pushed; at the last minute, he'd jumped. Jumped because the ocean was his only chance of getting away. If he'd remained on board, he would have been killed. That was a given.

He felt weak enough now that if someone had said he'd bled out and was dying, he would have assumed they were telling the truth.

"And you found me?" he asked, his voice as gravelly as that of a man who'd been smoking for seventy-eight years.

Beginning to realize that he *wasn't* on the cruiser anymore, he felt a compelling need to get the details straight. "And you brought me here?"

"Yes." She seemed to be studying him closely.

He squinted his eyes, taking closer measure of her. Granted his head was still throbbing and the wound in his chest kept shooting balls of fire, making it a struggle to speak, but something just wasn't adding up. This perky blonde looked as if she would have trouble holding up a large bouquet of flowers, much less dragging him anywhere. He weighed a good one-eighty. The woman did *not* look as if she could move that on her own.

"By yourself?" Who else knew he was here? And just where was "here" really?

"I had help," Stevi replied, her eyes

never leaving his face. This guy didn't seem threatening, but he wasn't exactly reassuring her, either. Had she made a mistake, bringing him here?

She couldn't help but wonder who was looking for him right now. Someone who looked like this, handsome even though he was bedraggled—and those green eyes of his, they were like two sparkling emeralds, luring her in—this was a person who didn't go missing without a lot of people taking note of the fact.

"Husband?" he guessed.

Stevi shook her head. "Gardener," she corrected.

"Why?"

Those eyes of his looked as if they could fish a confession out of a stone, she thought. If she tried to lie to him, she had a feeling he would be able to tell.

"Because he was there and he could be trusted not to talk until I wanted him to," she said honestly.

"No, why did you bring me here?" he stressed.

Again she wondered if she had done the wrong thing. But now wasn't the time to second-guess herself. Now was the time to try to get some answers of her own.

"Well, I couldn't just leave you on the beach," she told him. "You were bleeding—a lot. You probably would have died if I'd left you there."

"It's a bullet wound. Why didn't you call the police? Or at least call an ambulance and get me to the hospital?"

Since he had provided her with the opening, she lost no time in getting to the tougher questions. "About that—"

She didn't get a chance to finish asking before he answered. "Someone wants me dead."

"Someone," she repeated. That sounded incredibly vague. Weren't there any more details?

"Yes." It seemed as if he was struggling to talk. She didn't like to think that he was in a lot of pain—she'd have to do something about that. And soon. But first, she just had to find out if this guy represented a threat to her and her family.

"Do you know who wants you dead?" she pressed. She'd drag the information out of him, if it was possible. And if, for some reason, he was having trouble remembering, maybe she could help him reconstruct the scene.

Oh, he knew who wanted him dead, all right. Just now, reliving those last few minutes in his dream, he'd seen Larry Crenshaw's face vividly. But there was no reason for her to know. It would only put her in danger and that would be no way to repay her for her kindness.

His mind clearing a little even though his pain was definitely gaining on him, he was beginning to believe the woman.

"No," he answered stoically.

"Do you know why you were shot?"

She just wouldn't let up. *Yes, I know that, too.* "The less you know, the better," he said, the words sounding almost guttural to him.

"Oh, right, because if whoever did this

finds out you're here and comes to finish the job, if you manage to escape and he finds me, I can tell him I don't know anything and he'll just believe me and go away. Or," she said seriously, abandoning the cheerful, chirpy tone, "will he think I'm lying and just kill me instead?"

"You have a good imagination," he murmured, clearly fading.

His eyes were closing again. Her need for him to tell her what she wanted to know before he fell asleep warred with her concern that he may need more medical attention than she and Silvio could provide. Her need to know what she was getting into here by sheltering him won out.

"Yes, I do have a good imagination, and right now, I'm imagining that you're telling me the name of the monster who shot you—or at least *why* he shot you."

She missed her window of opportunity. Weak, obviously exhausted by his ordeal and worn out by the effort it took to talk, the stranger had lost consciousness again.

She sighed. She had nothing. Not his name, not the name of the man—or woman—who shot him, or any real details of what had happened to him or why. For that matter, she didn't even know if he was a criminal. Although there was still that feeling inside her, that feeling that had her convinced that he wasn't.

Could she really feel this certain if he *was* a criminal?

Or was it that she wanted an exciting romance to fill her life and suddenly, there he was, waiting for her and she was bending the facts to fit the fantasy?

"Well, at least I know you're not in a coma," she said, consoling herself. "Next time you wake up I'm going to keep you talking until you actually *say* something that makes sense. Although…I guess first I should try to get some food into you and get you strong."

A soft knocking on her door made her jump. She glared accusingly at the door. *Now what?*

Glancing one last time at her unexpected, incommunicative houseguest, she hurried over. "Yes?" she asked, without opening it.

"It is me," she heard a man say quietly, "Silvio."

Silvio.

Had he come to tell her that he'd notified the police even though she'd asked him not to? Or maybe he'd told her father. She wasn't sure which made her more nervous right now.

Stevi swung open the door quickly. "What are you doing here?"

Even as she asked the question, she grabbed hold of his wrist and pulled him inside, then closed the door behind him. While she didn't want anyone seeing him outside her door—there was absolutely no reason for her to be talking to the gardener in her room—she also wanted him to see their patient and reassure her that she wasn't hurting the guy by not rushing him to the hospital.

"Well?" she asked. "Is something wrong, Silvio? What are you doing here?"

He didn't say anything immediately. Instead, he looked past her toward the man sleeping on the bed. "I came to see if there has been any change. But I see he is still not awake."

Quickly she got him caught up on what had transpired since he'd left the room earlier.

Silvio was immediately on the alert. "Did he say anything else?"

"Just that the less I knew, the better." She felt somewhat defensive of the man, especially since he was back to not being able to speak for himself.

"So he told you nothing."

Excuses rose to her lips, but there was no point in trying to make the situation out to be better than it was. Silvio was right.

"Pretty much," she admitted.

His eyes pinned hers. "Now can we go to your father and have him deal with this man? He has a right to know that someone who is not a paying guest is here, in his daughter's room."

"Not yet, please, Silvio," she pleaded. "I know what I'm doing."

"Maybe you do, but I do not," he informed her. He spoke softly, as he always did, but his tone was unnervingly serious. "This is not right, Miss Stevi, having this man here like this in your room."

"Maybe not." She wasn't about to get embroiled in an argument about it. She needed Silvio as an ally. "But if you're worried about him…he can't do anything to me. He's much too weak. He tried to sit up and all I had to do was hold his shoulders and he couldn't budge. He's as weak as a kitten, Silvio. Really."

Silvio snorted. "If he were a kitten, I would not be worried," he said gruffly. He crossed over to the bed and glanced at the bandages he'd wrapped around the man's shoulder earlier. "I should change these."

"Got more right here," she volunteered, going into her bathroom and opening her medicine cabinet. She got out the alcohol again, as well as more bandages, and was back in a moment. "Were you a physician's aide for long?"

Silvio shrugged. "Long enough. It really is not important." Then, because she was waiting for a number, he gave her one. "Ten years." He glanced at her over his shoulder. "Why?"

"Because I think that anything to do with medicine is impressive and I'm just surprised you never told any of us about that before now."

"There was no need to before now," he said matter-of-factly as he removed the old bandages and began to disinfect the area again. "No one had been shot before today."

"True." She peered at his profile as he worked. "But why keep it a secret?"

"Why not?" he countered. "It is part of my past, my other life, and what I do here, at the inn, is my life now. I am not interested in the man I was, only in the man your father brought out in me."

She knew better than to ask him why he couldn't be both.

For now, she was just glad he had the necessary skills to save her mystery man.

CHAPTER SEVEN

"WHERE ARE YOU going to sleep?" Silvio asked. Finished rebandaging the stranger's wound, the gardener wiped his hands on a hand towel as he turned around to face Stevi.

Caught up in wondering about the unconscious man's identity and just how he came to wash up on her beach, Silvio's question seemed to come out of the blue and she wasn't prepared for it. It took her a moment to bring herself back into her sunny bedroom.

"What?"

"Where are you going to sleep?" Silvio repeated. "He is in your bed. That means you cannot be in your bed." It seemed a simple enough question as far as he was concerned. "Where will you sleep?"

She shrugged. She hadn't thought that far ahead yet. "I'll worry about that tonight." One glance at Silvio's face told her that he wasn't satisfied with her answer. "Don't worry, I'll come up with something. I promise."

He had no authority over her, but the situation as it stood still bothered him. "I still think we should go to your father and tell him about this man."

"We will," she assured him. "I just need to figure out how to approach him with this."

What she was really looking for was a way to get her father to agree to help, even though circumstances were a bit edgier than they had been when, say, Dorothy or Silvio had turned up at the inn, down on their luck.

"The truth should do it," Silvio told her matter-of-factly.

"Are you speaking from experience?" she asked.

Right now, she would have welcomed any input.

"We are not talking about me," Silvio pointed out. "We are talking about the man in your bed."

Despite the somewhat grave situation, Stevi laughed. "That sounds salacious."

"What?" He had come to English later in his life.

"Never mind." It had been a feeble joke, not worth repeating. "This will all work out, Silvio, I just know it," she said with confidence. "And I promise not to get you into trouble."

His eyes pinned hers as effortlessly as the odds-on favorite wrestler pinned his opponent. "It is not me getting into trouble that I am worried about."

She smiled and brushed a quick kiss on his cheek. "Yes, I know. Thanks for caring, but really, I'll be fine."

"When he wakes up again, call me," he told her, pulling a cell phone out of his pocket.

She looked at him in surprise. "I didn't know you had one of those. Good for you," she said, delighted.

For the most part, technology was something that Silvio tended to ignore or resist.

"It was a gift from your father. He thought I should have one. As if there was someone to call," he said more to himself than to her.

"Okay, I'll give you a call if he wakes up. What's the number?"

Silvio stared at the phone. "I do not know. Nothing is written on it."

Stevi put her hand out. "Here, give it to me. I'll find it."

She had a hunch Silvio hadn't turned the cell phone on—and he hadn't. When she proceeded to do just that, the cell's number briefly lit the screen.

Handing him the phone back, she said, "I've got your number. You want to write it down?"

"Why?" he asked uncertainly. "I would not be calling myself."

She laughed and shook her head. "I guess you have a point."

Pocketing his phone, Silvio moved toward the door and opened it. "You will call me?" he asked again, pressing the point home.

She raised her right hand as if she was taking a vow. "The second he opens his eyes and I get a chance, I'll call you."

Silvio appeared to catch the significant phrase buried in rhetoric. "See that you get the chance," he told her sternly.

She crossed to the door and eased it closed behind the gardener. "Yes, sir," she promised for the umpteenth time.

HER MYSTERY MAN slept for the rest of the day. Several times, uneasy about his condition, Stevi held a mirror up to his face to see if he was breathing. It was something she remembered reading in a short story once. At the time, she'd thought the trick was rather silly and ancient. Now she was glad she remembered since his chest gave the impression of hardly moving.

Stevi stayed in her room all day. She didn't want to take a chance on leaving and having the patient wake up while she was gone.

She was fairly sure that he was as weak as she had told Silvio he was, but there was always the outside chance that he would wake up and use whatever strength he did have to leave the inn. He was in no condition to fend for himself in the outside world and if, as in all good spy stories, whoever had tried to kill him should see him out and about, this time they might finish the job. She doubted very much if the man would be able to defend himself, as weak as he was.

So, to guard against that happening, Stevi remained in her room. She'd had the scrambled eggs and ham she'd brought for breakfast and when he didn't wake up, around one o'clock she had the plate of cold, somewhat soggy pancakes for lunch.

Throughout it all, she kept her eye on the stranger, fairly certain that he'd be awake by dinnertime.

He wasn't.

Silvio had not come by again and she

didn't want to impose on him, so she didn't call him. She also didn't have anything to eat for dinner. Stevi decided to tough it out, telling herself that skipping a meal once in a while wasn't a huge sacrifice. As long as nobody missed her and came looking for her—especially if Cris was making her big announcement to the whole family about her pregnancy.

She hesitated, then decided they'd never miss her in the loving chaos that was bound to erupt when the baby news came out. She didn't really want to miss that—she was happy for Cris, she really was—but she was so preoccupied with what she'd undertaken, she was afraid she'd draw attention from her sister.

She dragged two spare comforters out of the back of her closet to create a make-shift sleeping bag of sorts.

"Hope you appreciate this," she told her houseguest, climbing in between the layers of comforters.

She dozed rather than slept.

Several times during the night she

thought she heard her roommate stirring and she bolted upright.

But each time she thought she heard him, Stevi discovered him still sleeping.

He slept through the night.

She really didn't.

By morning Stevi felt achy and the worse for her impromptu sentry duty. Depleted of energy and yet oddly wired, she skipped her morning run, choosing instead to spend the time observing the man in her bed.

As time went on, she grew somewhat anxious. Maybe the reason he hadn't woken up all day was because he *had* slipped into a coma, she thought, becoming progressively more worried.

She forced herself to put her concerns on hold until after she showered and got dressed. This time around she cut her prep time by half.

When Stevi came out of the bathroom, she was disappointed to find that her mystery man hadn't come to.

She stood over him for several minutes,

debating what to do next. She didn't want to leave him like this and she definitely didn't want to take a chance on making his condition worse by just assuming that he was all right when he could very well not be.

If he was all right, wouldn't he have woken up by now?

Very gingerly, she shook his right arm. When there was no response, she did it again, a little more forcefully this time.

By the fourth attempt to wake him, she was shaking the stranger by his shoulders.

Even though she was trying to wake him up, when his eyes suddenly opened at the same time that he grabbed her by the wrist she was *not* prepared. The quick movement brought a gasp from her and a groan from him. It didn't take an Einstein to figure out that the searing pain had caught him by surprise.

"Morning," Stevi said with forced cheerfulness.

"You." With a sigh, he released her

wrist and fell back against his pillows. "So I didn't dream you. You're real."

"Absolutely," she assured him.

He looked around the room, vaguely remembering it from what he'd thought was his dream but obviously wasn't. What he wasn't clear about was exactly where he had landed. "And this is—"

"Still my bedroom in the inn," she said. "Before we go any further and you possibly pass out on me again, I need a name."

He looked blankly at her. "A name," he repeated.

"Yes."

His eyebrows drew together as a puzzled expression descended over his face. "You don't have a name?"

This was going to be harder than she'd thought. "*I* have a name. *You* don't have a name. At least, not one that you've given me."

He was still staring at her as if she was speaking some foreign language. Had the bullet wound scrambled his brain, as well? Loss of blood could do a lot of things.

Gamely, she forged ahead anyway. "I'll start you off. My name is Stephanie Roman. Everyone calls me Stevi."

He frowned. "That's a man's name."

"That's a subject for a different time," she told him rather than launching into an explanation as to why she and her sisters all had boy's nicknames. "Your turn. What's your name?"

He didn't answer her immediately. Instead, he took in a long breath as he looked around his surroundings again. The room had a great deal of sunshine coming in through filmy white curtains. The sunlight made the room look bigger somehow, despite the clutter. There were clothes waiting to be hung up, books waiting to be put back on the shelves lining part of one wall and a desk that had at least two layers of things piled on it.

This was not a room that belonged to a person with control issues. He turned back to look at her. "Is this your bed?"

She had thought that was self-evident. Obviously not. "Yes, but—"

"Where did you sleep?" he asked, feeling guilty for having displaced her.

"On the floor, next to the bed." She waved at the bunched-up comforters at her feet. "Stop changing the subject. Why won't you tell me your—"

"Ryan." The name emerged before she finished her question.

Ryan. Nice, she thought, nodding. "Okay, Ryan, next—"

"Mike." His head was muddled, he realized. He was doing this out of order.

She squinted, as if that would somehow help her absorb this.

"Which is it?" she asked. "Ryan or Mike?"

He closed his eyes for a minute. The room was beginning to spin and the sunlight that was streaming into it was hard on his eyes.

"Both. Mike Ryan," he told her. "My name is Mike Ryan."

That sounded almost fake, she thought. Until it was proven otherwise, she supposed she'd have to take him at his word.

"Okay, that wasn't so hard, was it?" she asked. Actually, it was from her point of view, but she didn't want to approach this with a negative attitude. The sixty-four-thousand-dollar question was still ahead. "Who shot you?"

He raised his green eyes warily to her face.

"I'm not sure."

Granted there had been a lot going on at the time, but he was fairly sure that he *did* know who had pulled the trigger. And that it was on the orders of Larry Crenshaw. But for now, he decided to keep that to himself because he still wasn't sure just where he was or who this woman was— who she worked for. And until he was sure, he needed to play it very close to the vest.

"Okay," Stevi said gamely. "Do you know *why* you were shot?"

Was she really just some beautiful Good Samaritan or was she pumping him to find out how much he remembered about the incident?

His memory of the incident that had almost been his undoing was crystal clear, but if he claimed ignorance, it might buy him a little time.

He went that route. "I don't remember."

She just looked at him.

After a beat, she said, "Yesterday, when I asked, you said the less I knew, the better. And now you're telling me you don't remember." She pinned him with a look. "So which is it?"

To be honest, he didn't remember saying that, but he took her word for it.

After thinking for a couple of moments, he said, "I didn't want to admit that I didn't remember. I thought it made me look stupid."

She supposed that could be plausible. And then again… "And you don't care if you look stupid today?" she challenged.

He shrugged his right shoulder. The other one appeared to want to mimic the movement, but pain prevented this… Mike…from moving it.

"I thought I owed you the truth, since

you've put yourself out so much for me. I guess that trumps looking stupid."

Stevi smiled. Finally, she was getting somewhere. Not a very productive somewhere, granted, but at least she was further along than she'd been yesterday. Baby steps, she told herself.

"Thank you."

Uncomfortably, he waved away her thanks. "Who else knows I'm here?"

"I was delaying the press release until this afternoon." When she saw the startled expression on his face, she felt guilty. "That was a joke," she said quickly. His expression returned to normal. She'd already labeled it "stoically good-looking." "Sorry, no jokes until you're stronger. Are you hungry? Do you want to clean up in the bathroom?"

As if in direct response to her question, Mike's stomach growled, reminding him that it had been close to two days since he'd eaten.

"Sorry about that," he mumbled.

"I'll take that as a yes to food," she said.

"I'll get you some breakfast. Anything in particular you'd like to eat?"

Food was food. He thought of it as fuel. "Whatever you bring back will be fine."

Stevi pushed aside the comforters on the floor for the time. She hesitated. "Promise you won't go anywhere until I get back?"

Mike answered her question with a question of his own. A rhetorical one. "You're bringing back breakfast, right?"

She flashed him a grin. "All right, then I'll be as quick as I can."

Stevi left, closing the door behind her.

Mike gave it to the count of ten. The door remained closed. Sitting up, he swung his legs out from beneath the covers. He was somewhat surprised, not to mention relieved, that he was still wearing his pants. That was one less thing he had to do, one less article of clothing he had to find.

Where was his shirt?

Scanning the room, he found it in a crumpled, bloody heap near the window, discarded by whoever had bandaged the wound in his chest.

Had that been her? Stevi?

Or the gardener she'd mentioned?

He liked the idea of her being the one who had seen to his wound far more than someone who spent the day with his hands in fertilized dirt.

"Probably owe my life to you, Stevi. Sorry I can't stick around to thank you properly, but having me around probably isn't safe for either of us," he murmured.

Standing up, his dizziness immediately intensified.

Struggling to keep upright, Mike took all of five steps away from the bed and toward the door before he felt his knees buckling beneath him. He began to bite off an oath, but the words vanished before they reached his tongue. Vanished as his knees met the floor.

By the time the rest of him hit the floor, he was out cold.

CHAPTER EIGHT

"I'D LIKE TWO breakfasts to go, Jorge. Same as yesterday," Stevi requested as she came sailing into the kitchen.

"Good morning to you, too," Cris called out as she glanced up from the steel prep table, where she was working.

Lost in her own thoughts regarding the man she'd left in her room, wanting to get back there as soon as possible because she wasn't really all that certain she could trust Mike to stay put, Stevi looked toward her sister in puzzlement. She'd heard her voice, but not what Cris had said.

"Excuse me?"

"I said 'Good morning,'" Cris repeated, articulating each syllable.

"Oh, right." Stevi flashed a lightning-quick smile in her sister's direction. "Good morning."

Cris frowned. "Are you okay?"

"Just fine," Stevi assured her breezily, then looked at her innocently. "Why?"

"Where were you yesterday?"

Stevi looked at her sister as if Cris had lapsed into gibberish. "What do you mean where was I? I was right here."

By that, it was obvious Stevi was referring to the inn. That wasn't what Cris was asking her sister. "I mean for lunch and dinner. You didn't come to the dining area, or to the kitchen. No one saw you," Cris added.

Stevi shrugged dismissively. She watched Jorge getting her order together. *Faster, Jorge. I'm getting the third degree here.*

"I was busy."

Cris stopped chopping green onions, laying her knife down on the chopping block. "Doing what?"

Stevi tossed her head. Her hair swayed about her oval face. "Do I ask you to account for every minute?" she asked defensively. "To account for every meal you make?"

"I wasn't asking you to account for every minute. I was just wondering where you were after running off with two breakfasts yesterday morning," Cris pointed out.

As if on cue, Jorge crossed over to Stevi and handed her a bag with the two breakfasts.

Thank you! Stevi thought.

Stevi gave the man a bright, grateful smile and said, "Thank you, Jorge. See you later, Cris."

The next moment, she was gone.

Cris looked after her departing sister even after Stevi had gone through the swinging door. With a sigh, she shook her head.

Turning toward her assistant, Cris asked, "Does she seem like she's acting weird to you, Jorge?"

Jorge busied himself with cleaning up his pans before going on to the next order that had been sent in. "Not my place to say."

"But if it was your place to say?" Cris prodded.

Jorge raised his dark eyes as he looked up at her. "Then yes, she is being unusual."

"Even for Stevi?" Cris asked. Everyone was aware that her sometimes overly sensitive, certainly impulsive sister took things to new highs at times.

Jorge gave her a long, penetrating look, then went on to prepare an elaborate Belgian waffle. "You already have the answer to that."

Yes, she did, Cris thought. She looked off in the direction her sister had taken and chewed thoughtfully on her lower lip.

Something was up, she thought. The question was: What?

STEVI HURRIED DOWN the hallway, hoping she wouldn't run into anyone before she reached her room. Or at least not run into anyone who would bombard her with questions, such as where was she going so fast, what was in the delicious-smelling paper bag, things like that.

She went as fast as she could without appearing to run, because that was sure to bring questions from even the most casual guest at the inn.

It wasn't until Stevi had closed the door of her bedroom behind her and turned that she saw him.

Saw Mike.

He was out of bed and lying facedown on the floor, in much the same position he'd been in the first time she'd laid eyes on him.

She didn't remember dropping the bag containing their breakfasts. Yet she was aware of rushing to his body.

"Oh, Mike, we have to stop meeting like this," she muttered under her breath.

Turning him over onto his back, Stevi attempted to rouse him again. This time she was successful. He opened his eyes.

"What happened?" he asked, dazed.

"You tell me," Stevi answered. "I left

you in bed. You promised me you'd stay there."

There wasn't a part of his body that didn't ache. It surprised him then, that despite the varying levels of pain he could still assess her features, still feel some sort of a pull toward his bossy guardian angel.

"I didn't want to inconvenience you any further," he told her.

She laughed shortly. "News flash, Mike, finding you on the floor like this isn't exactly an improvement. Here, let me help you back into bed."

Squatting, Stevi angled her body so that she could take his good arm and drape it over her own shoulders for leverage.

"No, that's all right. I can do it myself," Mike protested.

Except that he couldn't and the upshot of it was that he fell backward and she wound up tumbling down with him. Less than half a second into the maneuver, she had landed, splayed out on top of her wounded patient.

Stevie felt a flash of awareness, followed by a wave of embarrassment that made her cheeks burn.

This was *way* too much contact with someone whose name she'd just learned less than half an hour ago, she thought.

"Sorry, this isn't the way to get you into bed. At least," she stammered, tripping over her own tongue, "not the way we both want to get you into bed." That didn't come out right, either. "I'll stop talking now," she announced since he was laughing.

"Oh, please, don't make me laugh," he pleaded, still directly beneath her. "It really does hurt, you know."

She made no comment. "Okay, we're going to do this together on the count of three," she said.

"Okay," he agreed gamely.

Looking at her, he would have never guessed she was as strong as she was. And she was definitely even more attractive close-up.

Eyes on Mike, Stevi began to count off the numbers. "One—two—"

"Stevi?" Cris cried. "What's going on? Who is this man?"

"No wonder you haven't been out of your room all day," Andy chimed in, crowding in behind Cris. "Did you bring one for me?"

Thrown off balance by her sisters' unexpected entrance, Stevi barely stopped herself from pitching forward again.

Braced, she shifted her body, then jumped to her feet, instantly defensive. She hadn't heard them knock. Were they spying on her?

"What are you two doing here?" she demanded.

"We were worried about you. Who *is* this?" Cris asked, her eyes shifting toward the unidentified, rumpled man.

"Mike Ryan," he spoke up, introducing himself. They looked alike, the three women. It wasn't a stretch to figure out they had to be related. Sisters, most likely.

"I found him on the beach," Stevi said quickly.

"Wow. And I thought your seashell collection was getting out of hand." Looking from Mike to Stevi, Cris demanded, "What's he doing on the floor in your room?"

"He's supposed to be in my bed," Stevi said pointedly to Mike.

"In your bed? Are you nuts? And what was he doing there?" Cris's voice rose with every word.

Andy laughed under her breath.

Stevi ignored Andy. "He's supposed to be healing," she informed her older sister. "Now if you'll give me a hand here, Andy, we need to get Mike back into bed."

Andy looked to Cris for permission. "Is it okay?"

Stevi could tell exactly what she was thinking. Her baby sister was worried about it getting back to their father. This mess, whatever it was, was her doing, not Andy's. Andy got into enough trouble on her own without adding this to the mix.

"Cris, he's hurt," Stevi pointed out. "He was unconscious when I found him."

"If he was unconscious when you found him on the beach, just how did you get him into your room by yourself?" Cris asked. It didn't take a math genius to see that the height and weight factor were more than Stevi could have handled on her own.

She was not about to get Silvio into trouble for this.

"That's not important now," Stevi answered, dismissing the subject. "What's important is that he's hurt, and didn't Dad teach us to always help those in need? Well, Mike needs help."

Cris turned to look at the man the argument was about. She was starting to feel queasy again and her head was beginning to pound, but she still needed some basic answers.

"Who are you?"

"He already told you his name," Stevi said. "And he's hurt and needs help. That's all Dad knew about Dorothy when he took her in and gave her a place to stay. The same went for Silvio. And—"

Cris raised her voice to talk over her sister. Everyone knew Stevi could go on forever. "None of them were wounded," she stressed.

"Externally," Stevi insisted. "Internally, though, they all were—"

The argument was escalating. Mike raised his hand, drawing attention back to him. "Please, ladies, I don't want to cause any trouble. Just give me a minute to pull myself together and I'll go."

Cris turned to scrutinize the man more closely. If she succeeded in getting him to leave, then what? What happened to him?

"Do you have somewhere to go?" she asked Mike in a somewhat less than indignant tone.

Right now, he knew he couldn't go back to what had been his "home" for the past two years. They were probably waiting for him there in case he had survived. And he knew that he couldn't easily reclaim his former life—not that the agency would let him right now.

Moreover, he had no idea whom to trust. Someone had leaked information, blown his cover. Lying low here was his best and only option, but not if it was going to be the source of friction and trouble among these three women.

"I can find somewhere," he told Cris vaguely.

"How?" Stevi demanded. Turning toward Cris, she filled in the important blanks. "He has no wallet, no money, no credit cards. He doesn't even remember how he got hurt. How's he supposed to fend for himself if he can't even stand up?"

Cris sighed. Stevi was right. Her sister had managed to breach her outer wall to reach the part that was a pushover. She couldn't just toss the man out in this condition.

"You can stay here—until you get better," Cris qualified.

"I appreciate the offer, but I don't want to be any trouble," he protested.

"I think we're past that at this point," Cris told him. Turning toward Stevi, she repeated, "He can stay. But Dad has to know."

Stevi winced at the thought. "Cris—"

"He has a right to know. It's his inn."

"Dad said it belongs to all of us," Stevi protested. "That means one-fifth is mine. I can have Mike stay in my fifth."

Cris frowned and shook her head in complete disbelief. "I think you're wasting your time as an event planner. You should really think about becoming a lawyer. You could talk the ears off a brass monkey."

Stevi disregarded the sideways compliment. "I don't care about the ears on a brass monkey, I care about winning you over."

"You have won me over. He can stay," Cris repeated, looking at Mike, who had managed to draw himself up into a sitting position on the floor. "But that's my one condition. Dad has to know."

"Okay," Stevi agreed. "But can we take our time telling him?"

"Like when? Halloween?" Cris asked with a touch of sarcasm, her temper uncustomarily short.

"Labor Day?" Stevi countered, only half kidding.

"Stevi, he— Oh, Lord." Her eyes widened and suddenly her face looked very peaked, the way it had the other morning.

"Cris?" Andy asked uncertainly. "What's wrong?"

Cris didn't answer. Instead, she spun on her heel and rushed into Stevi's bathroom.

Andy started to follow her, worried that her older sister was going to suddenly be sick. She was startled when Stevi barred her way.

"It's okay," Stevi assured her—clearly Cris hadn't had that conversation with the rest of the family yet about her pregnancy. She sure hoped her sister had at least been able to tell their father when Jorge called him into the kitchen yesterday morning.

Andy looked at her as if she was crazy. "What do you mean, 'it's okay'? Cris looks as if she's going to throw up."

"She is," Stevi said.

She still remembered what Cris had gone through when she'd been pregnant with Ricky. She'd kidded her that she spent so much time in the bathroom, the post office was going to forward her mail there. Stevi hoped it didn't go as hard on her this time.

Andy still hadn't made the connection. "Then I should—"

"Andy, she's pregnant."

Andy blinked. "She's what?"

"Cris is pregnant. With child. Of the bun-in-the-oven persuasion," Stevi explained.

But Andy shook her head. "No, Stevi, you're getting her confused with Alex."

"Alex and Cris are *both* pregnant. Cris didn't want to steal Alex's thunder because it was Alex's first baby."

Andy struggled to keep her jaw from dropping. "Really?"

Stevi grinned as she nodded. "Really. I think she wanted to be the one to tell the family, though."

Holding on to the side of the nightstand, Mike managed to just barely drag himself into an upright position. The room still spun a little and waves of weakness kept insisting on washing over him, but he'd manage. He'd been in worse situations and somehow survived and even come out on top. This would be no different. All he needed was a couple of days of rest, but that was a luxury he wasn't about to find here.

Stevi suddenly realized what the man she'd found on the beach was attempting to do. Hands on her hips, she confronted him. "Just where do you think you're going?"

He tried once—in vain—to get around her. That failing, he tried reasoning. "Look, you people have enough going on. You don't need me around to complicate things."

"We're a fifth-generation bed-and-breakfast inn run by a man with four daughters. Trust me, we live for complications," Stevi said. "The complication we don't need is you passing out in our reception area."

He could understand that. It might make it difficult to explain to the guests. "I'll take the long way around, the way you said you did."

She stared at him, caught off guard. "How did you know that? You were unconscious."

"I heard you. You were talking in my sleep," he said, now realizing it.

Mike was perspiring, Stevi noted. His forehead was damp. She was *not* about to let him leave the inn in this condition.

"You're climbing back into that bed and that's the end of it, understand? Andy?" she said, shifting to look at her younger sister. "Help me overpower this guy and get him into bed."

Mike raised his right hand in surrender. He didn't have enough strength to fight off one of them, much less two, even though they looked like little wisps. He had a feeling they were sheer steel underneath.

"Okay, okay, you talked me into it. I'll stay put." Trying to climb back in, he all but collapsed into the bed, barely having enough strength to swing his legs in after him.

"Just what are you going to tell Dad?" Andy said.

A lopsided smile curved her lips. "He followed me home, Dad, can I keep him?"

Andy shook her head. "That's not going to work."

Moving around the room as she thought, Stevi was willing to admit that though whimsical, saying something playful to her father at a time like this was *not* the way to go.

"Didn't think so," she agreed, then said, "I'll tell him the truth. That I found Mike unconscious and hurt. Dad doesn't turn out anyone in need, right?"

"Right," Andy said, although she didn't look convinced.

"And Cris has already softened him up for us," Stevi continued as Cris came out of the bathroom, looking a wee bit worse for wear.

Hearing her name, Cris looked at her, waiting. "And how did I do that?"

"You told Dad yesterday morning that you're pregnant. You know what a push-over he is for grandchildren. How did he react?"

Cris quickly looked at Andy and then back. "Stevi! I didn't end up telling him because I decided I wanted to wait until my husband was with me before I told anyone and now you've gone ahead and told Andy? I can't believe you."

Oh, no. "Oops. Well, if I hadn't told Andy, she would've kicked down the bathroom door and then you would have had some explaining to do. Think of it as a favor I did you."

"Thanks." Cris rolled her eyes.

Andy was at Cris's side and hugging her before their expecting sister could lambaste Stevi any further. Then suddenly, they were all laughing and shaking their heads.

"This is great," Stevi said in realization. "Now you can tell Dad and he'll be shocked as well as happy. You'll soften him up and stun him all at once. What's one wounded man washing ashore on our beach compared to your wonderful news?"

Mike had remained silent for most of the exchange, feeling for the most part that it was best to speak only when someone addressed him directly. After listening to her, he now looked at the young woman who had rescued him with a new admiration.

She was devious and she thought fast on her feet. The agency he'd left in his past would have loved to have someone like her on their payroll. As for him, he was grateful she was in his corner. He

just hoped that neither one of them—
especially her—would regret this unfore-
seen alliance.

CHAPTER NINE

"WHAT'S UP? I CAME as soon as I got your message," Shane McCallister, Cris's husband for all of six months, said as he entered the kitchen through the side delivery entrance and crossed to her, nodding to Andy and Jorge as he passed and mussing little Ricky's hair affectionately.

He slipped a protective arm around the woman he'd known since they were back in high school. Brushing a kiss against her cheek, he asked in a lower voice, "Are you all right?"

Cris smiled at him, touched by his concern. "Except for horrible bouts of nausea, yes, I'm all right."

He quickly looked up at the others to see if they'd heard what she said, but Andy was picking at something sizzling on the stove while Jorge tried to shoo her back.

Of course he was glad that his wife was okay, but he didn't understand why she'd called him away from his construction project. The message he'd gotten on his voice mail made his appearance back at the inn sound urgent.

"Then why the 911-sounding call?" Shane asked, still not 100 percent convinced there was nothing wrong.

She turned into him, keeping her own voice low. "Because I wanted you here when I told my family—my dad, really—about the baby."

They had decided to make the announcement when the family was together for some special function. What had changed?

"Just like that?" Shane asked quizzically. "For no reason?"

Cris thought of the man Stevi had in her room. Where to begin the explanation? "Well, there's a little more to it than that," she admitted.

Where she had hesitated, her five-year-old, privy to more than he should have been, did not.

"Aunt Stevi's got a man in her bed," Ricky piped up. The boy was old enough to know that the situation was out of the ordinary, but too young to understand why.

"What?" Shane asked, bewildered. "What's he talking about?" He looked from his wife to Andy, his sister-in-law, who now joined their conversation, for an explanation.

Cris placed her hand on his chest. "Long story," she answered, then added quickly, "which I will tell you as soon as we tell my father that we're adding to his family tree."

By now Shane was thoroughly confused—not to mention that Andy and Jorge seemed to know that he and Cris were expecting a child…so he appeared to be late to the family announcement part of the revelation anyway. "What does one have to do with the other?"

This, at least, she could set straight for him. "Stevi thinks if we tell Dad about the baby, he'll be in a really good mood and then she can tell him her story," Cris explained.

Okay, now things were falling in place a little bit. Stevi had always been the unpredictable one in the family, Shane thought.

"If there's a guy in her bed, your father's not going to be overjoyed but I don't think she has to worry about him shooting the guy."

"He's already been shot," Ricky told his stepfather importantly.

Cris looked reprovingly at her son. No matter how hard she tried to keep him out of things, somehow Ricky always managed to wind up right in the middle, and he absorbed everything.

She sighed. "Little pitchers have big ears."

Ricky's face scrunched up as if that would help him understand what his mother was saying. "You mean like a baseball pitcher?"

This was getting her nowhere. "Just come," she said to Shane, taking his hand.

Shane looked around as they passed the reception area. "So where is your father?"

Still holding her husband's hand, Cris led the way down a corridor. Ricky skipped along beside them. "It's Andy's job to bring Dad and Alex to Stevi's room."

"Why can't we all meet in the reception area, or the veranda?"

"This is family stuff," Cris explained. "Dad wouldn't want one of the inn's guests overhearing—especially if he winds up having a meltdown."

"Meltdown?" Shane repeated. This was beginning to sound somewhat serious. "Your father's one of the most level-headed people I've ever met. He takes everything in stride."

She hoped that would continue to be true, but it didn't hurt to take precautions. "Everyone has their breaking point and Stevi can drive someone there faster than anyone else I know. Let's just say we're being cautious."

"So Stevi's trying to use our unborn baby as a shield?" Shane concluded, amused.

"Let's just say she knows what a softie Dad is when it comes to little people." Cris stopped walking and looked at her husband. Maybe she was taking too much for granted. "Are you okay with this?"

"Anything you want is okay with me," Shane assured her, giving the hand holding his a quick squeeze. "You know that."

Cris smiled at him as they turned down the hallway to Stevi's room. "Yes, I do."

She'd gotten lucky twice, Cris couldn't help thinking. Once when she'd married her first husband, Ricky's father, and once when Shane reentered her life last year. After Ricky's father had been killed in the service of his country, she really didn't think she would ever be able to love again. But then, she'd underestimated Shane's persistence. Thank heaven he hadn't given up on her.

"Can I tell Grandpa, Mama?" Ricky asked, shifting from foot to foot, looking at her eagerly. "Can I, please? I've been good and kept the secret like you told me to. I didn't say anything to Grandpa about our baby."

Cris found that part rather incredible, seeing as how it usually seemed as if words entered Ricky's ears and came out of his mouth almost simultaneously. She had never known him to keep a secret before and she had gone through a great deal of coaching to get him to promise not to say a word to his grandfather until they made their announcement.

Of course, she thought, amused, she'd only told the boy an hour ago. But for Ricky, an hour was an eternity if it involved keeping a secret.

"Yes, you did," she agreed, planting a kiss on top of the boy's head, and sharing a smile with Shane, nodding to reassure him that the news had gone over well with her son—his son now, too. "This is our secret to tell, Daddy's and mine," she reminded him. She was delighted that Ricky had taken so easily to calling her new husband his daddy.

"How come?" Ricky's eyebrows formed one wiggly, quizzical line. "The baby's in your tummy, not Daddy's."

"For now, but it's *our* baby, remember?" she corrected.

"For now?" the boy echoed, then a look of genuine distress came over his features. "It's not going into my tummy next, is it?" As if to make sure, he looked down at his T-shirt.

Cris pressed her lips together, struggling not to laugh out loud.

"No, you and your daddy are safe. I just meant the baby is part of the family so in that way, it's *our* baby," she explained.

Cris had never been so happy to reach Stevi's room in her life.

"Here we are," she announced, knocking.

"If you'd waited for the door to open the last time instead of walking in like that, you might not have had to drag your husband away from his job site," Stevi observed as she opened the door. "Hi, Shane. Sorry about this."

"No problem," Shane answered, looking over her head. He nodded toward the man on the bed. He was propped up with several pillows, his chest bandaged. What was going on, he wondered. "Who's that?"

Stevi beckoned her brother-in-law forward. "Mike Ryan, this is my brother-in-law Shane McCallister. Shane, this is Mike Ryan."

Leaning forward, Shane shook the man's hand. "Friend of Stevi's?" he asked the man.

Mike replied, "Might say she's a lifesaver. My lifesaver."

"What is all this?"

Richard Roman's gentle but authoritative voice was heard in the hallway. Stevi instantly spun around, alert. Braced. She took in a deep breath.

Showtime, she thought.

"Dad, Alex," Stevi began, addressing

the two latest arrivals Andy had brought, "Cris and Shane—"

"And me!" Ricky exclaimed.

Stevi flashed a quick smile at her nephew. "—and Ricky have something to tell you," she announced, plowing forward to get in front of her father. She was trying to divert his attention for as long as possible from what was in the room just beyond her sisters, brother-in-law and nephew.

Taking her cue from Stevi, Cris said excitedly, "We're pregnant, Dad."

"Really?" Richard cried, a huge smile bursting over his lean face.

"Really," Cris confirmed. "I'm a little more than one month along. About two weeks behind Alex," she added, glancing at her older sister.

"Cris, that's wonderful," Alex cried, grabbing both of Cris's hands in hers. "Why didn't you say anything sooner?"

Cris gave her the same reason she'd told Stevi. "I didn't want to steal the spotlight from you."

"Idiot!" Alex cried, pulling her sister into her arms and hugging her hard. "The spotlight's big enough for both of us." Alex went on to hug Shane as Richard, tears shimmering in his eyes, embraced Cris.

"I am so happy for you—and for us," Richard said into her hair as he held on to her. "And if my vision wasn't so blurred by these tears in my eyes, I'd swear there was a man in Stevi's bed." Releasing Cris, he stepped back, shifting so that he could embrace his son-in-law. "But that's just my eyes, playing tricks on me, isn't it?" Richard's question was directed toward Stevi.

There was no way around this. She had to face up to the truth.

"No, Dad, your eyes aren't playing tricks on you," Stevi said, praying for words that would make her father see her side.

Richard moved around the circle of family and approached Stevi's double bed and the man who was in it.

"Hello, I'm Richard Roman," he introduced himself as if finding a bandaged man here was an ordinary, everyday occurrence. "And you are…?"

"Very grateful to your daughter for saving my life," Mike said, thinking it was best to begin with that piece of information. "Mike Ryan, sir."

Attempting to sit up, Mike extended his hand toward Stevi's father. The loss of blood he'd suffered made him fall back against the pillows as if he'd just exerted a great deal of energy.

Richard turned to Stevi. "Did you get a doctor to look at him?"

"Not exactly," she hedged, not really sure how she was going to explain anything at all about this situation, much less work around incriminating Silvio.

She could have spared herself the concern.

Her father looked pointedly at the bandage covering Mike's chest. "Silvio did this, didn't he?"

Stevi's mouth dropped open. She was

stunned that her father would guess that right out of the box. Recovering, she rallied quickly, taking all the blame. It was the least she could do for the man who'd been her reluctant coconspirator.

"I made him do it, Dad," she told him. "Please don't be angry at Silvio."

"I'm not angry," Richard replied calmly. "I'd expect him to do nothing less."

If he noticed how surprised his words rendered everyone else in the room except for Ricky, who really didn't understand the exchange, Richard gave no indication.

Moving closer, her father pressed his long fingers against Mike's forehead. A satisfied expression slipped over his face.

"It doesn't feel as if you have a fever," Richard informed him.

Mike put his own meaning to the words. He was being told he was well enough to go. The nod he offered caused him a little dizziness but he struggled to disregard it. "I'll leave the inn if you just give me half an hour to get—"

"You're in no condition to be going

anywhere." He looked around for any sign of used dishes or discarded trays. "Have you been eating?"

Stevi spoke up. "I brought him food, but he's been asleep most of the time so he hasn't eaten since yesterday morning."

Richard frowned. "I thought as much. You need to eat, boy. Stevi will feed you if need be, but you have to build your strength. That's all you have to concentrate on right now," he said with a smile, patting the arm closest to him. "Getting stronger. Now, the rest of you," he said, turning to address his family, "leave the room. Give Mike some air to breathe. Stevi, you know what to do."

She looked at her father sheepishly. He had never been the kind of father who yelled first and thought things through later, but she had still been worried about his reaction to all this. She hadn't really expected him to be *this* understanding.

"Beg for forgiveness?"

"Feed your friend," Richard corrected.

And then his eyes met hers. "We'll talk later," he promised.

Maybe begging should have been the way to go, she thought.

"Is Aunt Stevi in trouble, Grandpa?" Ricky asked, wanting to know everything about everything.

Taking his hand, Cris pulled her son to her. "Ricky, hush," she chided.

"Yes, she is." Richard's answer to his grandson's question surprised the rest of his family. "She should have come to me right away," he told the boy, raising his voice just loud enough for Stevi to hear as well, as he walked out.

Stevi watched her family file out noisily after him. It wasn't an orderly retreat.

The whole scene made her smile with affection—as well as relief. That her father wanted to talk later was to be expected and at least he wasn't angry with her. And that was all that really mattered.

Once she and Mike were alone, Stevi pulled her chair closer to the bed again, then went to fetch the plate of scrambled eggs and ham to go that she'd had Jorge prepare earlier.

Sitting down, she looked at Mike. "You heard the man. You have to eat," she said, holding the plate in one hand and offering him a fork with the other. "If you can't do it yourself, I have no problem feeding you," she said. "Just say the word."

"Your father didn't ask me any questions," he said in amazement. "And despite that, he's still letting me stay here."

Things like that just didn't happen in his world. He operated in an atmosphere of constant danger, suspicion and mistrust. This almost seemed like a dream. It certainly wasn't part of any reality he was familiar with.

Stevi nodded as relief curved her lips into a smile. She had *really* thought that this time, she'd pushed her father's buttons. It just showed her how much she had underestimated her father.

"Dad's got a big heart."

"Runs in the family," he noted, once again thinking that he would have most likely been dead if she hadn't come along and helped him when she had. Someone else might have been afraid, especially once they saw the bullet wound. He was more grateful to her than he could possibly say.

"I'd like to think so," she said, assuming that he was giving her an awkward compliment. "Now then, are you up to feeding yourself?"

The idea of feeding him sent an appealing warmth through her.

Mike took the fork from her. "I'll feed myself, thanks."

But when he tried to pick up his first forkful of eggs, his hand shook so that very little remained on the utensil by the time he managed to bring it to his lips.

"Here," she coaxed, gently taking the fork from him. "It's hard to feed yourself with your hand waving like that. Let me give it a try."

"I hate feeling so helpless," Mike complained, frustrated as he watched her.

"You're not helpless," she argued. "You

just lost a lot of blood. That'll all be in your past once we get a little good food into you—and the food is all good here," she said, hoping her chatter would be enough to distract him as she fed him.

"Cris is the best chef around. You'll be bending steel in your bare hands by the end of next week."

"Don't want to bend steel," he murmured as exhaustion overtook him. "Just want to be able to use a fork."

"Decidedly less challenging than bending steel," she agreed. "Lifting a fork should fall into your bag of tricks in about a day. Day and a half, tops. You'll be feeding yourself with the best of them before you know it," she teased. "Now, here comes the plane, into the hangar…"

He was struggling mightily to fight off sleep and stared at her.

"What did you just say?"

How could he not know the plane into the hangar kid/food move? "It's a game we all played to get Ricky to eat," she said slowly. When she saw his blank look, she realized that she was tossing names around and he probably didn't catch anyone's earlier. "He was the short one in the room."

"The little boy," he said. "And he belongs to…?" Stevi slipped another forkful of food into his mouth.

"All of us, but technically, he's Cris's son. She was the one next to Shane. Tell you what, when you're stronger, I'll give you a formal introduction to everyone. But right now, all you have to do is eat and sleep, like my dad said."

That was when she realized that Mike had already taken her up on it. She sighed. "I guess you don't need much practice with the sleeping part, huh?"

Rising, she set the plate on her bureau and then crossed back to the bed. Very gently, she tucked a blanket around Mike.

"Sleep well, sweet prince," she murmured.

Well, Stevi thought, she could either sit here and watch him sleep, or seek out her father for that talk he wanted to have. And while the former really was tempting, she knew she really needed to get the latter out of the way.

"Okay, Dad," she said under her breath as she slipped out of her room and closed the door behind her, "let's talk."

CHAPTER TEN

As was her habit for the better part of each day, Alex was manning the front desk. Two guests—a couple celebrating their tenth wedding anniversary—had just signed in and were being shown to their room. The staff had spent the morning decorating the room to resemble a bridal suite, as per the husband's request.

Stevi made what turned out to be a vain attempt to get lost in the shuffle of suitcases and guests.

Alex saw her anyway.

"Stevi."

The second her older sister called out her name, Stevi pretended not to hear, but she braced herself nonetheless. Alex was the oldest, she was controlling to a fault on occasion, and in addition she was organized beyond all normal standards. Alex was also the one given to lengthy lectures, something Stevi was definitely *not* in the mood for right now—not that there was ever a good time to be on the receiving end of a lecture. Alex was known for her sharp tongue.

Alex rounded the desk and blocked her from what might have been a successful exit. For a pregnant woman, Alex was exceptionally quick on her feet.

"Stevi, I was calling you."

"Sorry, in a hurry to see Dad, talk later," she said, talking in sound bites in an attempt to add credibility to the urgency of her excuse.

"How's he doing?" Alex wanted to know, addressing the question to her back before she managed to get out. "The guy whose life you saved, how's he doing?"

The question ground Stevi's plans for a successful getaway to a halt and she turned around to look at Alex.

"He fell asleep again, but thanks for asking," she answered guardedly.

"But he is okay, right?" Alex pressed, her eyes pinning Stevi where she stood.

"As near as I can tell, yes," Stevi answered. "Why?"

Alex got down to the heart of the matter. "Just don't want the inn getting any bad publicity."

Stevi wasn't sure she followed her sister's reasoning. "Come again?"

"Well, if he died here, that wouldn't exactly have guests flocking to the inn for summer vacation and this *is* the start of our busiest season."

Retracing her steps, she came closer to Alex, not wanting their conversation to be overheard by anyone.

"He's not going to die," Stevi retorted. "Silvio took care of him—did you know that Silvio had medical training?"

"Not specifically, but I don't think I'd be surprised by anything he did. I don't know his backstory," she added quickly when she saw that Stevi looked as if she was about to ask for details. "All I know is that he grew up in Argentina and that his wife and son left him—although that might have been part of his cover."

Confusion highlighted Stevi's features. "What do you mean, his 'cover'?"

Alex grinned. "Well, you know. When we were younger, I was the one who used to think that Silvio had a mysterious past like Zorro."

"Didn't hurt that he sort of looked like a slightly older Antonio Banderas," Stevi added.

"Then you remember how we used to imagine that maybe he was with one of those alphabet agencies. You know, CIA, DEA, NSA, bureaus like that, and they had turned on him."

"Right," she said. "Or like Cris used to believe, maybe he found something that made him turn on them."

"In any case, you know everything I know—he showed up here one night, trying to figure out his next move. Turns out, his next move was to remain here and help Dad with the garden. Anything else you want to know, you should ask Dad when you have that talk with him. Although, good luck with that—he's never given us any details when we asked in the past."

"Right. The talk." Stevi looked over her shoulder. "Is he in his office?"

Alex nodded. "The last I saw, yes. If he's not, don't worry. He wants to talk, so he'll find you."

Stevi sighed. "I never doubted it for a minute."

Like a soldier bracing for a dressing-down—or a demotion in rank—Stevi marched over to her father's small office.

The nine-by-twelve converted alcove was located just off the reception area, tucked in next to the kitchen.

More than an office, it was her father's private refuge. She suspected that after her mother had died, her father had come here to let his guard down.

Her father kept up appearances, she knew, for their sake. If they collapsed and cried, their father would be there to make it all better for them.

But who did he have to depend on when their mother died? Stevi now wondered. And now, even when his best friend and Wyatt's father, Dan—the man she and her sisters had grown up thinking of as an uncle—had died, she knew that her father had come here, to his office, to close the door and be alone with his thoughts and his memories and just possibly, to pretend for a little while that life was continuing just as it always had, with her mother and Dan in it.

She didn't like intruding on him when he was in the office with the door closed, as it was now. But he was the one who wanted to talk to her so she felt that she had to interrupt his solace.

All it took was one quick knock.

Her knuckles had hardly touched the wood before the door opened and her father was standing in front of her.

"Hi," he greeted her as if they hadn't just been together a little while ago in her room.

"You said you wanted to talk," she said. "So here I am."

"Come on in," he invited, gesturing. When she crossed the threshold, her father closed the door behind her. Indicating the chair in front of his desk—an antique desk that had been handed down from generation to generation, right along with the inn.

Stevi perched on the edge of the chair, ready to spring to her feet if need be.

Sitting down himself, her father leaned back in his chair and observed his third-born. "You can relax, you know. I'm not preparing to drag you over hot coals—twice."

If possible, she sat up a little straighter. "I know that."

He went on to tell her, "I wanted to ask for a few details about Mike."

"That's what I have," Stevi said, forcing a cheerful note into her otherwise nervous voice. "Just a few details. Very few," she emphasized. And then, before her father could say anything more, words began to spill out of her.

"He was just lying there yesterday, Dad, on the beach, when I was jogging back to the inn. He was bleeding and he grabbed my wrist and said…" She hesitated. What he'd said was "No police," but she didn't think her father was ready to hear that…. "He said, uh, 'Help me,' then he passed out. I couldn't just leave him there," she cried, then doubled back on her sentence when she realized it wasn't factually accurate. "Well, actually, I did leave him there—"

He tried to stop her. "Stevi—"

"—because I went to get someone to help. I was going to get you, or Shane, but I saw Silvio first, so I asked him and at first he didn't want to—"

He tried again. "Stevi—"

"—because he felt it was being disloyal to you, but I convinced him he had to come and he brought his truck so we could get Mike up to the inn and—"

"Stevi!"

Stevi stared at her father, startled into silence. She couldn't remember the last time she had heard him raise his voice—to anyone.

After a beat, she asked, "What?"

"Breathe," he ordered. When she looked bewildered at the instruction, he added, "Now."

Stevi nodded and took in a huge breath, her eyes riveted to her father's face. He signaled that she needed to take in another breath when she let the first out, so she did, still keeping her eyes on her father. Her breathing became more regular.

"Better?" he asked.

Stevi nodded. "Better. I was just trying to explain how Mike got into my room."

"I really just wanted to know if you'd ever seen him before you came across him on the beach."

"No. But I—"

Her father held up his hand to stop another possible flood of words.

"You don't have to explain anything else. I understand that you saw someone who needed help and you helped him. Considering that I've been doing that myself all these years, I can't really fault you for doing the same thing, now, can I?"

Stevi pressed her lips together, then began to frame a reply. "Well—"

She never gave up, he thought fondly. Stevi was his scrapper. "That didn't really require an answer, Stevi."

She exhaled another long breath. "So you're not angry?" she asked, still carefully watching him for a sign that perhaps she'd assumed too much.

"For following the example I set for you?" he repeated. "How could I be?"

Relieved, Stevi grinned broadly. Her father was a terrific guy and she could think of nothing worse than offending him enough to get him angry with her— or worse, disappointed with her.

"And, Dad, please don't blame Silvio for anything," she added. "I asked him not to tell you. He wasn't very happy about it. I could see that he really felt terribly disloyal about that."

"I don't blame Silvio for anything," Richard said honestly. "Silvio is nothing if not loyal." For now he left it at that. Stevi didn't need to know that it hadn't taken Silvio all that long to make up his mind as to where his loyalties were aligned. "He's a good man."

Since they were talking about Silvio like this, Stevi had a burning desire to know more about him. It had been nagging her since she'd watched the gardener sew up Mike's wound.

"What's Silvio's story?"

"What do you mean?"

"Well, he sewed up Mike's wound like a pro. I watched him," she added.

Richard smiled. "That's because he is a pro," he confirmed.

She wanted to be sure she and her father were on the same page. Something still felt off. "Then he *was* a physician's aide?"

"Is that what he told you?" her father asked. There was a touch of surprise in his voice. The corners of his mouth curved slightly. "I see."

She was into nuances. The inflection in her father's voice negated her initial belief. "Then he wasn't a physician's aide?"

Richard paused for a moment, reflecting. "Silvio was a doctor in Argentina. A doctor who didn't believe that medicine should take sides in a civil war. There were others who didn't quite see things his way. When he saved the wrong person's life, he had to flee for his own. Silvio lost everything," he concluded quite frankly.

She remembered that story. That much hadn't changed. "You mean his wife and son, right?"

Her father inclined his head. "In a way. They left before he had run for it. His wife, he told me later, sided with the opposition. She was angry that he didn't take advantage of certain opportunities that had come his way, choosing, instead, to honor his Hippocratic oath. She told him she could do better. The next day, she and his son were gone."

While she'd known he'd lost his family, she'd never heard the exact particulars before. Hearing them made her heart ache for the man.

"Oh, poor Silvio," she murmured. Being deserted after choosing to do the honorable, right thing had to have devastated the man.

"Don't ever let him hear you say that," her father cautioned. "Silvio won't stand for pity—from anyone." He knew how fond the man was of his daughters, especially Stevi, who was the closest in age to his own son. Having her pity him would have been a huge blow to Silvio's pride. "What I just told you was something he told me only after he'd been here for several years. It's not for general knowledge," he warned.

"Why did he tell you all of a sudden, out of the blue like that?"

"I wondered the same thing," her father admitted. "He told me that it was his son's birthday. My guess is that he just missed him more than he could stand and needed to talk to someone."

Stevi shook her head. "I can't picture Silvio needing to talk to anyone, much less confessing something. Can't see him missing anyone either, even if it was his own son."

Richard smiled. It was the sort of smile that was forged out of years of hard living and even harder lessons.

"People have a way of surprising you, Stevi," he said.

She nodded absently, her mind already moving on to a bigger problem. "What do you want to do about Mike?"

"Do?" he repeated. "We allow him to heal. Once he is healed, we'll see what happens after that."

She nodded, rising. That sounded more than fair. That meant that she had to be fair to her father. Which in turn meant that she couldn't leave until she was sure that he had been made aware of one fact.

"That wound he has, the one that Silvio

stitched up—" She stopped for a second, took a deep breath and then forged ahead. "It's a gunshot wound."

Her father nodded. She couldn't decide whether he was just being calm for her sake, or he already knew what she was telling him. "Does he know who shot him—and why?"

Stevi shook her head in response. "He says he doesn't remember."

Richard's eyes met hers. "Do you believe him?"

Stevi paused for a moment, not because she was trying to decide whether or not she believed Mike's story, but because she was surprised that her father was waiting to hear her evaluation of the situation.

"Yes, I believe him," she answered.

That was all he wanted to hear.

"Okay, that's good enough for me, Stevi," he said. "So we wait until he heals and regains his strength. And maybe, if he's lucky, his memory will come back to him, as well."

Instead of leaving, Stevi came around

the desk and pressed a kiss to her father's cheek. "How long have you been taking in strays, Dad?" she asked him fondly.

The man really *was* simply the best, she thought.

He laughed softly.

"For as long as I can remember, Stevi," he replied. "For as long as I can remember."

CHAPTER ELEVEN

WHEN STEVI RETURNED to her room after talking to her father, she found Mike awake and attempting to sit up.

"Hold it, don't strain yourself," she cautioned, hurrying over to the bed. She was afraid that if he tried to do too much too soon, he might wind up tearing his stitches—or something worse.

"Trying to sit up isn't supposed to be straining myself," Mike protested.

This was all his doing. He'd let his guard down for a second and all this had happened because of it. Now here he was, being taken care of by a slip of a thing. It wasn't right.

Yet there was no denying that he felt rather shaky right now and he just wasn't used to it. He'd always been the strong one. This was a whole new experience for him and he didn't like it at all.

"We'll have a debate about that later," she promised him, bending down so that she was approximately level with his shoulder. "Here, lean on me and we'll see about getting you comfortable."

Mike definitely wasn't happy about needing help—hers or anyone else's—but he recognized that it would be a lot easier doing it Stevi's way than being stubborn about it and struggling to drag himself upright on his own.

Besides, Stevi smelled like wildflowers. And there was something rather nice about having her softness support him.

Once he was more or less in an upright position, Stevi quickly lodged pillows behind his back to keep him that way.

"There," she said triumphantly, taking a step back. Satisfied, she looked at him and asked, "Ready to try it again?"

He had no idea what she was talking about. Did she have some sort of an agenda after all? Maybe she wasn't as innocent as she looked.

"Try what again?" he asked guardedly.

"Eating. You fell asleep before I could get very much into you," she reminded him, then laughed. The sound made him think of delicate wind chimes. "I figure at this rate, you'll be done with breakfast just before Christmas dinner." Not that she minded playing his nursemaid. "So, ready for more?"

Mike shrugged. "I'm really not all that hungry," he admitted.

It did strike him as odd, seeing how he hadn't eaten since before his near-fatal chest-meets-bullet, diving-into-the-ocean-to-survive encounter, but his appetite was nonexistent.

"Too bad, you need to eat," she informed him, mustering as much authority into her voice as possible. It was a lot easier trying to boss Andy and Cris around than this man, even if it was for his own good.

He stared down at the plate she brought

over. Eggs and ham. "I guess better that than a bowl of oatmeal," he rationalized.

His comment struck a chord. "You don't like oatmeal?"

He made a face in response. "I won't tell you what it reminds me of. Suffice it to say I absolutely hate oatmeal."

"Huh. Small world," she commented, then said, "Me, too. When I was a girl, my mother tried every way she knew how to get me to eat oatmeal, bless her. But it didn't matter what she did to it, how she sweetened it, I just couldn't get myself to actually put a spoonful into my mouth and swallow any of it down." She shuddered just to think about swallowing the thick, pasty cereal. "Now then, I'll give you the same choice I gave you before. Do you want to feed yourself or would you rather that I did it?"

He took the plate from her and rested it on his blanket. "I think I'm strong enough to lift a fork."

As he began to eat, there was a quick knock on the bedroom door. Before Stevi could murmur a frustrated, "Now what?" the door opened and Cris walked in carrying a tray. There was a covered dish on it and from the aroma, whatever was under the cover was fresh and hot.

Cris nodded at Mike and said, "I thought something hot might be more appetizing. So I put together a doctor-approved hot lunch for you. Broth, Jell-O, warm biscuits, nothing too heavy for your digestion until you get used to eating again." She set the tray down on the bureau. "Let me know if there's anything you'd like to have me prepare." She glanced over her shoulder at Stevi. "Bring the tray back when you get a chance," she requested. Then, telling Mike, "Don't eat too fast," Cris left the room.

"Cris treats everyone the same way she treats her son, Ricky," Stevi explained.

They each had their skills, their attributes, the one thing they did better than the others, and they brought it to the table, to try to help others—and each other—whenever they could.

"It's the mothering instinct," Stevi continued. "Cris seems to have it in triplicate for some reason. And now that she's pregnant again, all I can say is that we're all pretty much doomed."

Taking away the by now very cold eggs, Stevi brought over the tray that her sister had carried in.

The fog in Mike's head was beginning to clear, thanks to all the sleep he'd gotten, and while his body was still depressingly weak, he *was* able to think straight.

About a lot of things.

And he knew what he was being confronted with was something out of the ordinary—at least in comparison to the day-to-day world he lived in.

"Are you people always this willing to put yourselves out for a total stranger?" he asked. "Not that I'm complaining, but I don't get to meet many people like you and your family. I'd say you were all unique."

Having given him the tray, Stevi made herself comfortable on the chair that was still at his bedside. She was hoping to finally be able to find out something about him.

"Where?" she asked.

He looked at her and shook his head, confused. "Where what?"

"Where is it that you meet people? Where you work? What is it that you do?"

The life he'd led for the past twenty-four months had trained him to assume a persona that would fit whatever occasion he found himself in and still sound believable to whoever he was talking to at the time. It was second nature to him and he slipped into it now.

For safety reasons, he became a man who couldn't readily remember anything beyond his name. He did *not* want to repay these people for their kindness by lying to them—especially to Stevi, but he'd been truthful with her earlier when he'd told her that the less she knew, the better.

His world was a dangerous place and

the sooner he got well and left the inn, the better off everyone else would be.

So, until he could make that happen, feigning ignorance was the best path for him to take right now.

He looked at her with all sincerity and said, "I don't know." He paused, allowing frustration to enter his voice. "It's all just a fog. Every time I try to remember, to recall anything beyond my name and a few simple facts, I find myself staring at this murky fog that won't let me break through." He sighed and then confided, "It's so frustrating."

Moved, Stevi nodded, completely sympathizing with him. In a rather small way, she understood. When she'd been in high school, she'd played a number of different sports and during one of the games— a soccer semifinal play-off—she'd been knocked to the ground and hit her head. She was out for what felt like forever. It had been more like five minutes but the upshot of it was that she couldn't focus on anything for almost two days.

The spill, even what she had done just prior to the contact that had sent her sprawling to the ground, eluded her.

"Don't worry, it'll come back to you," she said. "It might take some time, but you'll be able to remember everything that's important." She really hoped that she wasn't just whistling in the wind in this case.

Mike nodded solemnly as if he was taking in every word. The small smile he offered her hid what was at this point a growing, rather large tidal wave of guilt.

Lying was his business, almost his vocation. He did it to stay alive, to do his job and to ultimately bring in what he referred to in his mind as "the bad guys."

But in this case he was lying to the good guys, to people who were putting themselves out for him. He knew he had to, that it was necessary, but that still didn't make it right or wash away his guilt.

And as such, it was hard for him to reconcile the two halves.

"By the way," Stevi pointed out, "don't

feel as if you have to clear your plate. Just eat what you can."

Wrestling with his moral dilemma, doing his best to attempt to beat it back and contain it, he nodded absently. He was only half listening. "Good to know."

Mike took a few more bites and began to feel drowsy again, despite his long naps. He was asleep before Stevi cleared the tray.

"Well, that didn't take long, did it?" she noted, looking at Mike. "Was it something I said?"

This time, she felt she could leave the room without fear that he might try to hobble away. She felt fairly certain that she and her family had put all his concerns to rest. Moreover, she had made a breakthrough with him and he trusted her. It was obvious that getting shot had put him in a position of not trusting anyone, so she was rather satisfied that she had made decent headway with him in that area.

Stevi stood there a minute longer, the

tray in her hands, watching him sleep. Without concerns to mar his features, he looked to be only a little older than she was. All sorts of questions popped into her head. Very few of them touched on who would want to shoot him and why. Mostly she wondered who he had been before this happened to him, before he had washed up practically at her feet.

And she wondered how long he would remain here before his memory returned and his life called him back.

Stevi sighed. One step at a time, that was all she could take. One step at a time.

Even so, for the first time in more than twenty-four hours, Stevi could feel the tension in her body beginning to leech out of her.

"Stay put," she instructed softly to Mike, then turned and using the point of her elbow against the doorknob, she opened her door and walked out still holding the tray.

She closed the door with her back and then headed off to the kitchen.

Walking in through the swinging door, she placed the tray on the long steel table.

Since it was between meals, Jorge was taking a break, as were the two part-time people helping Cris prepare and serve during lunch and dinner. Cris was the only one in the kitchen when she walked in. Her sister was busy working on a menu for the next day.

Preoccupied, Cris still glanced up when she heard the tray meet the tabletop.

For the time being, she set the menu aside. "How's the patient?"

"He likes your food," Stevi told her. "Thanks for bringing it."

Cris waved away Stevi's thanks. There was no need for it. "No problem. But that's not what I asked. How is he?"

Stevi gave her the complete rundown. "Weak, tired, frustrated because he can't remember things—like what he did for a living and why someone would have taken a shot at him," she explained when Cris looked at her quizzically regarding the source of Mike's frustration.

"Hopefully, that's just temporary." Still, Cris knew that wasn't a foregone conclusion. There might be complications that weren't being addressed. "You know, maybe Dad should call Doc Jacobs. Doc still has some hospital privileges, doesn't he?"

The man she was referring to was a retired physician who was also a long-time friend of their father's. When their father had fallen ill, years ago, it was Doc who had laid all their fears—and there had been a slew of them—to rest.

Maybe it wouldn't hurt to have the man look at Mike now, just to be sure, Cris thought.

"I think so," Stevi said in answer to Cris's question. "But to be honest, I get this feeling that Mike would rather just try to get better on his own. But if he doesn't improve in a couple days, then maybe we should override him and look into having him see someone official."

"You mean other than Silvio," Cris guessed with a grin.

Stevi nodded. "Yes." She hesitated for a moment, wondering if Cris was privy to the information her father had just given her. "Did you know that according to Dad, Silvio was a doctor?"

The way Cris's eyes widened, she realized that her sister didn't know. "You're kidding, right? A doctor? *Our* Silvio?"

Stevi nodded, telling herself that she wasn't saying anything that Cris wouldn't have eventually pieced together herself. "One and the same."

The revelation clearly took Cris by surprise. "Maybe we should ask Dorothy what she did before she came here. For all we know, Dorothy might have been an international spy."

"Now that's really reaching, Cris," Stevi said with a laugh.

But Cris wasn't all that sure she was wrong. "I read somewhere that Julia Child was part of the OSS at the end of World War II," she said, referring to the precursor to Britain's MI6. "So, who knows? It could have happened," she speculated.

The very idea made Stevi laugh harder. "Maybe you're right. That earth-mother look of Dorothy's would be the perfect cover for a spy." And then she sobered a little as she thought of Silvio again. What else had the man she and her sisters had thought of as a guardian angel from time to time done? What other skeletons were buried in his closet? "I guess you just never know about a person, do you?"

Cris readily agreed, then said as her sister began to leave the kitchen, "Just don't you go keeping any more secrets from us, deal?"

Stopping, Stevi flashed Cris a grin. "Deal. But that works two ways, you know."

Cris looked at her, bewildered. Her life was as transparent as they came. "I don't keep secrets," Cris protested.

The expression on Stevi's face said she knew otherwise. "What do you call being pregnant?"

"Oh. That. I call it wonderful," Cris answered with a wide smile. "And now that you all know about it, I am free to be deliriously happy in public."

She looked at Stevi as a thought occurred to her. Here she was, happy beyond her wildest dreams, her life beautifully mapped out before her, and Stevi's life was still very much up in the air. She wanted for Stevi what she had. A man to love who loved her back, a son—and a baby on the way. It was, all in all, the perfect life. She wanted the same for Stevi.

"Think he'll stay on?"

The question came out of nowhere and for a moment, Stevi had no idea what her sister was talking about—or whom. They'd just been talking about her pregnancy, so she made the only logical association—except that it wasn't all that logical from where she was standing. "Are you talking about the baby?"

"No, you idiot, I'm talking about Mike."

The next moment, she was struggling to bank the warm feelings that were flaming inside her. "Why would he stay on?"

Cris pointed out the obvious. "Silvio

did. Dorothy did. Jorge just took this as a temporary job and he's been here for three years now. The inn is kind of a haven for lost souls, so I thought that maybe, if it turns out Mike was trying to get away from something, being here might give him a fresh start—and he'd stay."

"I'm sure once he pulls himself together and fills in the blanks in his memory, he'll go back to his life," Stevi told her sister, doing her best to sound as if she didn't care one way or the other.

But she did.

THE SEED THAT Cris had planted with her question quietly took root within her as Stevi walked back to her room. She needed to take some of her things and move them—and herself—into the adjoining room the way her father had tactfully suggested just before she left his office. But that wasn't the foremost thing on her mind right now.

The idea of Mike remaining, of his staying on as someone who contributed in some way to the inn's day-to-day existence, became more and more captivating with each step that brought her back to her room.

Back to Mike.

For pity's sake, get a grip, Stevi. Your Adonis probably has a Mrs. Adonis, or at least a significant other, waiting for him someplace, maybe even looking for him right now. When he gets his memory back, he'll be back to his old life like a shot. And you are going to be left out in the cold with a lot of wistful thoughts and a handful of memories, if you're lucky.

She knew that. Impulsive though she was, she was also practical if that was called for. She knew the odds were against his remaining at the inn; knew, too, that the odds of regaining his memory were in Mike's favor.

But until then, she thought as she opened her door and slipped back into her room, her eyes drawn to the sleeping man, she was going to enjoy every second.

Until it was over.

CHAPTER TWELVE

HE WASN'T SURE what woke him.

One moment, he was in the midst of a dreamless sleep, the next his eyes were wide open, his brain trying to process whether the noise he'd heard had been in his sleep.

Or in his room.

Mike had bolted upright before he knew what he was doing, reaching for the gun beneath his pillow—that wasn't there.

Then he remembered where he was.

The room wavered just a little. Or maybe that was him. He'd been mending slowly these past few days, far slower than he'd wanted to. Yet, he had to admit, progress was being made and at least he was still alive.

Whenever he became impatient or frustrated with himself, all he had to do was remind himself of the alternative.

He still had no idea what it was that woke him, but he took it as a sign that he was finally getting back to normal. Because of the nature of his work, he'd trained himself to instantly wake up if a strand of hair landed on a rug.

He'd done it because his life could very well depend on it.

At least, it had until he'd found himself on that cabin cruiser with Larry Crenshaw and the cartel kingpin, Ortega, not to mention a full complement of men on Ortega's payroll.

And then it came to him. He knew what had woken him up.

Rain. The sound of rain hitting a windowpane.

Sitting here in the dark bedroom, listening to a rare summer storm wind down, it was almost hard to believe that people like Crenshaw and Emilio Ortega even existed.

It was as if he'd fallen down a rabbit

hole and wandered into a storybook land where kindness and manners counted and a person was measured by the way he could make someone else's day better rather than by sales figures quoted in kilos and the number of drugs exchanging hands.

He didn't bother turning on the light. The dark was soothing and he'd gotten accustomed to using it to his advantage.

Getting out of bed carefully, Mike made his way over to the small, sliding back door and opened it. A fine mist greeted him, landing like small, welcoming kisses along his face.

The miniscule balcony looked out on the back lawn and beyond that, he could make out the ocean. It looked like undulating velvet from where he stood.

The water seemed restless tonight, he noted.

"Welcome to the club," Mike murmured under his breath.

"Something wrong?"

Her voice startled him, but he kept

his reaction in check, another habit he'd picked up, thanks to the cartel. Instead, he looked calmly in the direction the voice had come from.

"What are you doing up?" he asked Stevi.

Wearing an oversize Chargers jersey, she was standing on the balcony in the room next to his. Her smile seemed to weave itself under his skin. He chalked it up to his somewhat fuzzy brain.

"Funny, I was just going to ask you the same thing," she said.

He tried not to notice how short her jersey was, but it wasn't easy. "Something woke me up. You?"

"Same. Except I think that most likely my something was you."

He was rather certain that he hadn't made any noise, but he wasn't going to argue the point with her.

"Sorry, didn't mean to wake you up. I thought I was being quiet."

"Quiet tends to make me uneasy," she confided, aware how strange that probably sounded to him, especially when she added, "Noise puts me to sleep." Stevi grinned at him. "So, are you up for the night?"

The answer was probably yes. "Why?"

"Because if you are, I'll come in. We can play cards. Or raid Cris's refrigerator. Or, if you're up to it, we could go for a walk along the beach. The rain's stopped," she pointed out. "We might need a flashlight. Although given the sky tonight, we might not."

The last suggestion had her grinning. Or at least her voice sounded as if she was grinning, because he couldn't quite make out her face. She was in the shadows.

"It might be nice to see you upright on the beach," she said.

He smiled. "I'm up to it," he told her. "Might be kind of nice at that."

"Okay, I'll meet you outside my—your room," she corrected herself, "in five minutes."

Mike changed, putting on a pair of jeans and a T-shirt that one of Stevi's brothers-in-law—Wyatt—had given him. Changing into them now reminded him of all the hand-me-downs and donated clothes he'd worn as a kid. When he got a job and earned enough money to finally buy himself his own clothing, he'd felt as if he was on top of the world.

Nothing had beat that feeling—or had matched it—since.

Running his hand through his hair in lieu of combing it, he slipped out of his room—and found Stevi standing in the hallway in front of the room, waiting for him.

"You're ready," he said in surprise, not bothering to hide it this time.

"I said five minutes." Stevi glanced at her watch. "It's closer to five and a half now."

He laughed and shook his head as he fell into place beside her and they headed out the back way, across the veranda.

"Listen, I know I'm the one who suggested going on this walk, but the second—the very second—you start to feel tired, or even anticipate getting tired, I want you to tell me, understand?"

"And what? You'll carry me back to the hotel on your shoulders, piggyback style?" he asked.

As they walked, the ebbing and flowing waves seemed to be playing a game of tag with their footwear.

"No, we'll turn around and go back to the inn. Unless you're suddenly too exhausted and then we'll sit it out until you feel up to walking back."

He wasn't used to anyone concerning themselves with his welfare or his comfort. It made him somewhat uncomfortable—because he found himself responding to it. "Don't you have anything better to do than be my babysitter?"

"Nope, not at the moment," she said cheerfully. "Certainly not at two in the morning," she added. Then, in case he thought that he was ultimately keeping her from something, she explained exactly where she was in her life when she'd found him. "I'd just graduated college and was busy finding myself when I tripped over you. Right now, I'm leaning toward thinking of you as my senior thesis."

He didn't so much as break into a smile.

"Don't tell me that you broke your sense of humor when you washed up on the beach."

"Why, would that be a bad thing?" he asked absently, staring down at the water as they walked, thinking about that night when it had all gone drastically wrong.

"It would be a disaster," she said without any hesitation.

Mike looked up, her tone bringing him back to the moment.

Abruptly, Stevi stooped down to pick something up. He almost tripped over her but caught himself just in time. The woman should have come equipped with turn signals and hazard lights.

"Nothing sees a person through hard times better than a sense of humor," she continued, straightening again. "It's what differentiates us from animals. We can laugh at ourselves."

"Hyenas laugh," he pointed out.

She shook her head. As she spoke, she brushed sand off the object she'd picked up. "Hyenas make a noise that sounds like they're laughing. We are the only ones who can actually laugh."

"I stand corrected," he acknowledged. Idle curiosity had him nodding at what was in her hand and asking, "What's that?"

"It's a seashell," she told him, holding it out to him. "Here."

He took the small shell from her and used what little light was available to examine it. The shell, appearing grayish in color, was rather small and compact. Not the most exotic seashell he'd ever seen.

He handed it back to her and she put it in her pocket.

"What are you going to do with it?" he asked.

"I'll add it to my collection."

"You collect very plain seashells?" he asked. "Why?"

"Well—" she hesitated "—maybe it's

something to remember tonight by. It's better than having nothing, in the end."

He shook his head. Stevi had a romantic nature and that was something he'd never been able to indulge in. Though he'd lived in the state all his life, beaches had not been part of his childhood. Learning to swim had been a sudden, last-minute needed skill before he'd gone undercover. Lucky for him, he now thought. Otherwise he would have been somewhere far below the surface by now.

"You know what? You keep this one," she said, fishing it back out of her pocket and forcing him to take it. "Marvel at the resourcefulness of the sea creature that used to live inside it. Like you, this seashell washed up onto the beach from somewhere in the ocean. Or just toss it back into the ocean and forget all about it. Maybe you don't need a keepsake to remember me—us, the inn—when you leave."

Mike looked at the shell. It was more intricate than he'd first realized. There were swirls and tiny ridges along its outer sides. He ran his thumb over it several times.

"It's rather pretty," he commented. "Might be good to have something pretty to remind me of…this place."

"I think so," she agreed. They began walking again and she noticed that he slipped the hand with the shell into his pocket. "There was a time I had an extensive seashell collection, but Alex got on my case, saying that if I kept on picking up every shell I came across, pretty soon there wouldn't be any room for me in my room. About the tenth or eleventh time she brought it up I knew that I either had to stop collecting seashells—or go on listening to her lectures."

She shrugged, thinking that maybe she should have stood her ground—it was the principle of the thing more than the shells themselves. But like a lot of things, that was in the past. "It was easier to stop. After that, I lost interest for a while and scattered the seashells, sending them back into the ocean." An amused smile curved her mouth. "Who knows? Maybe the one in your pocket used to be one of mine."

He could just about make out the curve of her mouth in the light from the half-moon. His fingers curved into his palm as he suppressed a desire to trace the curve with his fingertips.

"Is Alex the oldest one?" he asked.

"Yes. Alex is also the control freak of the family. You're laughing," she said, surprised. "Why?"

"Because I have a feeling that if anyone else called her that—me, for instance— you'd be all over them."

Stevi shrugged. She thought about denying his assumption, but then, looking back, she knew that she couldn't. They had always had each other's backs when it came to outsiders, even in the middle of an argument. "I guess you're right. An outsider hasn't earned the right." She didn't think she was saying anything unique. "Isn't it like that in your family?"

He laughed shortly, then shook his

head. He looked straight ahead, focusing on the ocean and the way it shimmered beneath the crescent moon. "No."

Was it her imagination, or was there hurt in his voice? "Oh, I'm sorry, I didn't mean to sound as if I was prying."

"You're not," he said, absolving her. "And there's nothing to be sorry about. I don't have one."

Stevi came to an abrupt halt and looked at him. "You don't have a family?" she questioned. "Or is it that you don't re-member having one?" He did, after all, admit to having trouble remembering some details. Maybe his childhood was part of those details.

"I don't have one," he clarified.

"What happened to them?" The ques-tion tumbled from her lips before she could stop herself.

He avoided her eyes, mainly because he wasn't certain how he would react to sympathy or pity and he now knew her well enough to know that both would be there for him to see. He wanted neither.

So he looked over the top of her head as he answered, "I have no idea. As far as I know, I was always alone."

That almost sounded as if he'd raised himself on the streets. Someone must have seen him and taken him in, or had the system look for a home for him, right? "Were you placed in foster homes?"

He'd been placed, all right, but as far as the word *home* went, that took more doing than just putting up four walls.

"Same thing," he replied.

"I am sorry," she said.

Why did she feel this need to douse him with sympathy and apologies? Served him right for giving in to a weak moment and sharing this with her. He shouldn't have said anything. The problem, he acknowledged, was that she was very easy to talk to. He was going to have to watch himself more carefully.

"Why?" he asked. "You didn't have anything to do with it."

"I can still be sorry," she pointed out gently. "Sorry that you didn't grow up

having siblings to fight with and to love."
A couple of steps later, she stopped walking again. In the darkness, he could just make out her serious expression.

Mike looked around, curious what had caused her to stop this time. Everything seemed completely the same. "What's the matter?"

"I think we should turn around and go back." They'd been walking for a while now. "I don't want you getting tired out."

Now that he was finally outside, he wasn't quite ready to go back. Inasmuch as he was very accustomed to being a loner and did better on his own, he liked this new feeling of solitude—solitude with her.

"I'm fine," he assured her.

She wasn't all that sure. She knew the male of the species didn't admit to fatigue—until it was painfully obvious and present. "Until you suddenly find that you've run out of energy and then I'll have to find a way to get you back to the inn."

"I'm not tired," Mike insisted. He'd

never had anyone fuss over him like this before and it felt strange, unusual and just the slightest bit…warming. Actually, he realized that there was a lot about this exuberant woman with the flashing blue eyes that he found rather appealing.

He watched her mouth as she spoke and found himself captivated by the movement rather than by what was being said.

Accustomed to digging in when she was trying to prove a point, Stevi did just that. "Well, I say you are and since you have no way of proving that you're not, you'll just have to—"

She didn't get a chance to finish her sentence.

One minute, she was standing toe to toe with Mike, the next, their toes were not the only things that were touching.

She knew a second before it happened that it was coming.

It occurred in slow motion and yet, at the same time, it happened quicker than a heartbeat.

Mike cupped the back of her head,

tilted it ever so slightly back and then, his eyes on hers, pressed his lips to hers.

What began as a simple proof to show her that he wasn't tired turned into something a great deal more. An awakening in both of them that they were not simply just two people, but that they belonged to two very distinct, opposite genders. Opposite genders who were acutely aware of one another.

Stevi found that her breath had suddenly, inexplicably backed up into her lungs and then stubbornly remained there just as the pulses in her temples, in her wrists, in the hollow of her throat, went into a beat that was more than equal to double time.

Breathless and growing more so, she caught herself leaning into his kiss. Into him.

Her heart was racing so hard, she was afraid it would race right out of her chest.

Mike had taken the initiative, wanting to show her that he was alive and well and quite happily on the mend. He was not only up for a longer walk, but in all likelihood, would be able to be out of their hair and on his way in another few days. What he actually wound up doing was proving to himself that perhaps he was not quite as energetic as he was pretending to be.

Kissing her had all but drained him even as it set his heart hammering—or maybe *because* it had set his heart hammering, that had made him feel drained.

Which came first, the chicken or the egg?

When he drew his head back, he found that he was somewhat unsteady and needed a moment to collect himself. A moment to pull the world back into focus.

"I guess maybe you aren't quite as tired as I thought you were," Stevi told him, doing her best not to suck in air in his presence and look like some sort of hopeless idiot.

A half smile took over the corners of his mouth. "Funny, I was about to say that maybe you're right. Maybe I was pushing too hard here."

Her eyes rose to his. "Maybe we're both a little right," Stevi said.

"Maybe," Mike agreed.

She grinned up at him, secretly glad he was taking the stand that he was. It meant that he was going to stay at the inn a little longer. And maybe, by staying a little longer, he might just decide that remaining at the inn wasn't such a bad thing. After all, others had done it before him.

She was suddenly very happy that she hadn't taken off for New York a couple of weeks ago.

Look what she would have missed.

Hooking her arm through his, she urged, "C'mon, let's go back."

"Took the words right out of my mouth," he replied.

They turned around and walked back to the inn, their steps rhythmically in sync.

CHAPTER THIRTEEN

EVER SINCE HE was sixteen years old, Mike had held down one job after another. Some had been manual labor, some had been white-collar.

If he thought about it now, it was hard for him to actually remember a time when he was *not* doing some sort of labor, whether or not he was compensated for his efforts.

He certainly hadn't been allowed to just sit around, doing nothing, in the various foster homes he'd been farmed out to. There was always, always something for him to do to earn his keep, as one foster parent had told him.

As he recalled, that particular foster parent had worked him extra hard—and showed his displeasure in extreme ways when the job hadn't been done to his satisfaction.

Consequently, Mike didn't do sitting around well. *Relaxing* was not a term in his vocabulary.

So once he was at least well enough to be able to walk along the beach with Stevi, he very quickly found himself at loose ends. He wanted to be able to do something to repay these people who were feeding him and putting a roof over his head, neither of which they were in any way required to do.

Nor were they asking anything in return.

All in all, Mike found the Roman family to be the most decent group of people he had ever had to deal with. There were no hidden motives, no mysterious agendas, and best of all, he didn't have to watch his back. No requirements of any kind, other than for him just to get well.

For someone like him, accustomed to having to deal with the dregs of society as well as those who dwelled in the underbelly of that society, Stevi Roman and her family seemed just about too good to be true.

Except that they were.

He found them not only to be a breath of fresh air; staying here at their inn was, for him, a vacation of the soul.

A vacation, he knew, that needed to end as soon as he was well enough.

But until then, he intended to enjoy being around them—around Stevi—as much as possible. And while he was here, he wanted to try to repay them for their hospitality in any way that he possibly could.

It was this restless need, this desire not to be in debt, that brought him into Richard Roman's office this morning after breakfast.

Asking the older man if he had a moment, Mike had come in, closed the door and stated his position to the head of the family.

Richard leaned back in his chair as he studied the young man for a long moment.

He was impressed. He'd had a good feeling about the young man when he'd first met him and it was only reinforced now.

Richard's chair creaked in protest as he shifted slightly in his seat. "So you're asking me for a job at the inn?"

"No, not a job, exactly, sir," Mike corrected, afraid that he wasn't getting his thoughts across very well. "Work is a more accurate description."

Richard's eyes never shifted away. "And the difference being?"

"Well, for one thing, people get paid for doing a job. They're doing something on a regular basis." He wasn't getting this right, Mike thought. His tongue was tripping him up. He tried again. "It has some sort of a sense of stability to it."

Richard cocked his head. "And you don't want to be stable?"

He knew this wasn't coming out right, Mike thought. "It's not that, exactly, but once I've regained my strength and get to feel like my old self again, I'll be leaving, so this is only going to be a temporary job, not something I intend to keep once I'm really back on my feet."

"I see." Richard nodded as he continued listening to him.

"Until then, though, I would like to repay you a little for the kindness you and your family have extended to me."

Richard smiled and shook his head. "That's not necessary, son."

"It is to me, sir." There was no wavering on this point as far as he was concerned. "I always repay my debts."

"Very admirable, Mike." His computer emitted a high-pitched beeping noise. Richard turned down the volume. "But this isn't a debt. If you feel you need to classify it, what's happening is more in the realm of a good deed. The only way to repay a good deed is to pass it forward. Do something helpful for someone else when the occasion arises and that's payment enough as far as I'm concerned."

Mike nodded. "I understand that, sir, and that's a very good philosophy. But until I get a chance to pass it on, I'd still like to show you my appreciation."

A strange pattern was beginning to reoccur on his monitor. Richard tapped several keys to erase it, but it stubbornly refused to disappear. "What did you have in mind?"

Over the years, because Mike had never had anyone to depend on but himself, he'd gotten rather handy in a number of areas.

"Whatever you need to have done, I guess. I'm pretty handy with tools," he volunteered. "If you have anything that needs fixing…" His voice trailed off, leaving it to Richard to fill in the blank.

But there were no blanks to fill in. "Right now, everything is in good working order, thank goodness. And when it's not, Shane, Cris's husband, usually takes care of it. He's good with things like plumbing or any major or minor electrical problems."

Richard frowned at his computer screen, doing his best not to allow it to distract him. But lately, he'd been involved in more than one battle of wills with his desktop.

"I'd have you give Silvio a hand with the garden work," he told the young man, "but I'm afraid he'd take it as an insult. Oh, nothing personal," he was quick to interject. "Silvio would think that I'm subtly telling him he's getting too old for all that heavy lifting and tedious labor. I wouldn't want to offend him for the world."

"Neither would I," Mike agreed. He had another suggestion. "I wouldn't mind any kind of maintenance work that needs doing, sir." In his time, he'd done everything imaginable on that level, including cleaning out a pigeon coop one of his foster parents had. "Cleaning, sweeping—"

With the mention of each chore, Richard shook his head. "I'm very lucky that way. I have it all covered." The monitor screen abruptly lost its picture, then just as abruptly, flashed an odd pattern across the screen. *"Everything,"* he repeated, all but gritting his teeth, "except this annoying machine."

Punctuating his statement, Richard hit one of the keys on the keyboard harder than was warranted.

The sigh he emitted seemed to come from the bottoms of his toes. He was not, by nature, an angry man, but his computer was really trying his patience of late.

"This is one of the greatest inventions of all time," he told Mike, never taking his eyes off the screen, which now seemed to be going from one site to another without any rhyme or reason. It also was increasing and decreasing its font size, apparently at will. "But when it decides it has a mind of its own, it makes me long for the days of the typewriter."

Maybe he had finally found something he could do for the man, Mike thought. "Problem, Mr. Roman?"

Richard threw up his hands. "It's beyond a problem. It's gotten to the point that it's decided to eat parts of the data that was inputted six months ago and now it's attacking next month's booking schedule, as well as giving me a headache."

Mike came around and looked over the man's shoulder at the computer screen.

"Do you mind, sir?" he asked Richard, nodding at the keyboard.

Richard raised his hands away from the keys as if to give up all claim to the infernal machine. "Be my guest," he said as he vacated the swivel chair. Mike took his place.

Despite owning and working on a computer for a number of years, Richard was still pretty much a two-fingered typist. That was not the case with Mike. The second he sat down he began typing at lightning speed.

"I think I found your problem, sir," Mike told him after a few minutes. The sound of his fingers hitting the keys underscored his statement. "You've got a virus."

Richard, of course, knew viruses were out there, and that—like human viruses—you didn't want to catch one. But he was only vaguely aware of this strange new electronic world he found himself wandering in. He took his cue more from Mike's tone that this was serious.

"A very bad virus?" he asked, watching Mike's expression.

Mike nodded, although he never stopped typing. "I'm afraid so."

"Is it fatal?" Richard asked. If it was, he had a problem. He hadn't budgeted for a new computer system. Six months from now, no problem, but right now, he was committed to an air-conditioning overhaul and that would take all the available cash in his business account.

He supposed that money could be found somewhere.

If Wyatt caught wind of the problem, there'd be a brand-new computer on his desk in less than twenty-four hours, but that wasn't the way he wanted to operate his business. He didn't want Alex's husband to feel that the inn was his responsibility in any way, no matter how fond his son-in-law was of it. The financial responsibility was his and his alone.

Mike glanced at the man who had taken

him in without firing questions at him, without demanding any sort of proof of identity or any explanations whatsoever. Richard also hadn't questioned his request not to report the nature of his wound to the authorities. That would bring up more questions than he could answer. More important, it would place him on certain people's radar. Radar he couldn't afford to be on right now. Not until he knew exactly who he could and couldn't trust.

It was better just to have everyone in the dark until he was strong enough to defend himself—as he knew he would be called on to do soon.

It wasn't a matter of if, it was a matter of when.

"Your computer tower's not dying on my watch," he told Stevi's father. There wasn't a hint of a smile on his lips when he said it.

LESS THAN FORTY-FIVE minutes later, Mike had gotten rid of the virus, defragmented the hard drive, then reformatted it—after backing up all the computer's files first. He also eradicated the problem of the ever-changing font size and the whimsical website merry-go-round.

"Try it," Mike encouraged, getting up from Richard's seat.

He turned the chair to face Richard. The latter sat down almost hesitantly, as if sitting was some sort of a commitment and he wasn't altogether certain exactly what it was that he was committing to.

But when he pulled up the screen he'd previously been trying to work on, he discovered data that had been missing—or winking in and out on an ever increasing, not to mention annoying, basis—for a few weeks.

He was greatly relieved.

Looking up from the monitor, he turned toward Mike. "What did you do?"

"I fixed it," Mike replied in his customary, noneffusive manner.

"Obviously," Richard agreed, pleased. "You're nothing short of a magician. Whatever debt you think you owe me, consider it paid in full."

And then the older man paused, as something occurred to him.

Mike was immediately aware of the slight shift in demeanor. "What?" he asked.

"Are you any good with printers?" Richard asked. "It won't print."

Mike tried not to laugh. "That covers a pretty wide spectrum of possible problems. Let me take a look at it."

"It's over there," Richard prompted, pointing out the offending piece of machinery by the opposite wall.

Twenty minutes, several replaced cartridges and one realignment later, the printer was up and running, as well.

"Nothing short of a miracle," Richard declared, looking down on the test page in his hands. "Maybe this was what you did for a living before your accident," he suggested.

They had all taken to referring to what had happened to Mike as an accident.

Mike preferred it that way, but he had a feeling that no one, especially Silvio, who was still keeping a close eye on him, believed that what had happened to him fell under the heading of an accident.

For his part, he didn't confirm or deny. He certainly never went into any details about it, maintaining that he couldn't remember what had transpired, or even how he had come to be shot. He'd told Stevi he couldn't see himself as being anyone's intended target.

She had looked as if she'd believed him at the time. Or at least believed that that was what *he* believed. He'd felt pretty guilty about deceiving her and the rest of her family.

The feeling kept compounding.

It was ironic, really. He was a man who lied for a living, lied to *keep on* living, and yet this white lie of his, created more to protect her and her family than him, ate away at his conscience.

"Maybe it is," Mike agreed, going along with the man's suggestion.

Being part of IT was as good a choice of careers as any. In choosing it and displaying his skills at resurrecting a computer and the malfunctioning colored printer, he had, purely by accident, created the perfect cover for himself.

At least it would keep Stevi from asking any more questions out of the blue, questions that he couldn't afford to answer.

"You've certainly saved me a great deal of grief," Richard said, heartily shaking his hand. "I like to think of myself as a very even-keeled man, but there's something about this computer when it decides to go on the fritz that just brings out the worst in me."

Mike laughed. Electronics had been known to bring out the very worst in even the most mild mannered. "You're not alone in that, Mr. Roman."

"If by chance I run into another glitch?" Richard paused. "If I do, would you mind if I called you to come help—provided you're still here, of course." They both knew that he was free to leave whenever he felt strong enough to do so.

But, on the flip side, there was no urgency for him to leave if he chose to stay.

"I'd mind if you didn't," Mike said.

"Then for as long as you choose to stay here, son, consider yourself on call as my IT guy," Richard told him with a chuckle.

"Absolutely."

He hadn't the vaguest idea why that would make him feel good. Better than he had felt, actually, in a very long time.

Except for that walk along the beach in the moonlight with Stevi.

That simple act had not, he realized, just rejuvenated him but, for a very small space of time, it had almost propelled him into a parallel universe, one where he got to experience all the things that he hadn't experienced in this one. The list included a normal childhood, high school proms… innocence.

A quick rap on the door had both men looking in that direction. Stevi stuck her head in.

The second she saw him, she grinned.

"There you are," she said with a sigh of relief. "I thought maybe you decided to take off without saying goodbye."

Was that what she thought of him? That he would just get it into his head to disappear without a word? Things like that wouldn't have bothered him before his stay here, but now, inexplicably, they did.

"I wouldn't do that," he told her quietly. Athough, he realized, he would've done that the first couple days he'd been here. In a heartbeat. But a lot had changed since he first woke up with Stevi watching over him.

"I might just decide to chain him to my desk," Richard spoke up. "Mike fixed my computer and the printer."

Mike shrugged. They'd saved his life. The trade-off was completely off balance.

He owed them far more than he could ever repay.

CHAPTER FOURTEEN

"YOU KNOW YOU don't have to do any of this, right?" Stevi asked, looking up at the man she found herself growing progressively closer to with every passing day.

She was standing at the bottom of a twelve-foot ladder, holding up another streamer for him to hang. The Fourth of July was a week away and decorating the grounds for the celebration was slightly behind schedule. She blamed herself for that.

When Mike had seen her bringing out the various boxes that housed the decorations she'd accumulated over the past few years, he'd insisted on taking over, despite the fact that he was technically still convalescing.

He looked down from the fourth rung

of the ladder. Amusement curved his mouth. He'd found himself smiling more and more. He felt unusually happy. Especially for a man recovering from a gunshot wound who knew that once the gang he'd failed to infiltrate found out he was still alive…well…let's just say the happiness was unexpected.

But then, what he'd been experiencing these past few weeks was a great deal different from the life he was accustomed to.

"You're not exactly holding a gun to my head here, Stevi, so yes, I know."

Hammer in hand, he was nailing red, white and blue streamers to the temporary posts he'd put up for her earlier. Leaning over to the side, suddenly he caused the ladder, uneven on the grass, to move slightly.

Alarmed, she made a quick grab for it, using her body to keep the ladder steady and upright. She looked up. "Are you all right?"

"I'm fine."

He would probably say that with his

dying breath, Stevi thought. Some men were just macho that way.

She was having trouble tamping down the waves of guilt she was feeling because she'd let him take over like this. At the root of it all was the fact that she liked having him around and this way, they'd be working together until the celebration took place.

Unconvinced by his assurances, she told him, "I wouldn't want you suddenly pitching forward. Maybe you should come down and let me finish putting up the streamers and the lanterns."

Mike made his way down the ladder, but it wasn't to hand over the hammer to her. He wanted to get another handful of nails.

"Anybody ever tell you you worry too much?" he asked, taking the nails and slipping them into the pocket of the borrowed jeans he had on.

"You want that chronologically or alphabetically?" she answered.

Mike laughed. "Then I'm not the first."

Yes, you are. You're the first one who's ever lit up my world. The first one I've ever thought about spending forever with.

Stevi pressed her lips together, knowing she couldn't say any of that out loud. If she did, she'd come across as a clingy, needy woman. That wasn't the way to induce him to stay—if he was inclined to, which she doubted. Most likely, since she wouldn't give voice to her feelings, once Mike was his former self, he'd leave, never knowing how she felt about him.

Maybe it was better that way. At least she wouldn't hear him say something along the lines that he was flattered that she liked him—or some such mindless drivel—but he was sorry, he just didn't feel the same way about her that she felt about him.

And why should he? Just because they'd kissed? Men and women kissed each other all the time. It didn't necessarily have to mean anything.

Except that to her, it had.

It did.

But that, she thought, was strictly her problem, not his. She was enough of a realist to recognize that. And enough of a romantic to hope that his departure date was somewhere further down the line.

"Were you really going to tackle all this by yourself?" he asked. Back up the ladder, he hammered in some of the nails he was going to need to hang her lanterns.

It wasn't because she liked being in charge, the way Alex did. It was a matter of working with what she had. Or, in this case, what she didn't have.

"Well, Alex and Cris are busy and besides, they're pregnant so I wasn't about to ask them to pitch in. And Andy, whenever she actually is around, is supposed to be watching Ricky. I've used up my next six months' worth of goodwill with Silvio," she said, glossing over the fact quickly, "and I'm not about to have Dad on a ladder, so that just left me."

"And me." Mike came down a couple steps. He extended his hand toward her. "Need more nails," he told her.

She didn't even bother looking into the box she'd brought out. "I seem to be out," she informed him.

She wanted him down off that ladder. Blessed with a vivid imagination, she could just see him reaching out like that again and this time, sending the ladder over onto its side. She wanted him to stay longer, but not because he'd reinjured himself.

Mike looked down and gave her a penetrating look. He'd just taken several nails out of the box and knew for a fact that there were at least several dozen nails of varying sizes left.

"No, you're not."

Stevi stuck out her chin. "Are you accusing me of lying, Mike?"

That would have been the word for it if he hadn't gotten to know her the way he had.

"I'm accusing you of being overprotective. You want me coming off this ladder so that you can scamper up it instead.

Now then, nails, please," he said, putting out his hand again.

Reluctantly, Stevi gave him several more nails. "And for your information, I do not scamper."

He laughed at her indignant protest. "Sure you do," he told her. "Someone as light as you scampers when they move." He paused his hammering, looking down and regarding her closely for a moment. "What do you weigh, ninety-five, a hundred pounds maybe?"

She weighed a little more than that, but her weight had been a sensitive issue for her when she was younger and she hadn't quite managed to conquer that fully yet.

"That's a conversation for another time," she said dismissively.

Ever since she'd found him in her father's office, asking for jobs to do, he'd been working almost nonstop on one thing after another. That couldn't be good for his healing process and even though it might ultimately hurry along his departure, she didn't want him doing anything to risk his health.

"Look, if this is about that debt you think you owe my father, you've already paid it back in spades. You fixed my dad's computer and his printer. Cris told me you programmed her tablet to operate faster and more efficiently so she could input her menus on that and I'm not sure how, but you seem to have won over Ms. Carlyle— and she does *not* take to strangers well. Whatever you did, she's a fan now. I overheard her singing your praises to Wyatt the other day."

The retired schoolteacher and Alex's husband became friends when he interviewed the woman extensively for the book about the inn he was completing. A book that had been initially started by his father. Knowing he wouldn't be able to see the project through, Dan Taylor had asked Wyatt to complete it.

Ms. Carlyle turned out to be a font of untapped information about the inn because she had been coming to it for literally decades.

"I carried her tray to her room the other morning when she wasn't feeling up to dining in the dining room," Mike said simply.

"Ah, then you rode to the rescue," Stevi told him, putting it into the chivalrous kind of language that the older woman would have appreciated. "She responds well to that. So, everything and everyone, apparently, is running smoothly thanks to your efforts. Ergo, there's no need for you to keep on repaying a debt that's already paid up."

Mike inclined his head. "Your father referred to it as doing good deeds."

"Okay…" Her voice trailed off as she waited to see where he was going with this.

Mike climbed down the ladder. He needed to move it farther along, to the next post. Because Stevi was slow to step back and give him enough room, they wound up filling each other's space again.

For a brief, heart-stopping moment, she thought he was going to kiss her again, the way he had that night on the beach.

But they weren't shrouded in darkness this time. Moreover, it was eleven o'clock in the morning and they were out in broad daylight when anyone could happen by and interrupt them.

The moment disappeared.

"I almost stepped on you," he commented as she took a step back belatedly.

"Almost," Stevi agreed, her voice subdued as she took another step back, doubling the space between them—enough so that he could move the ladder without hitting her.

"Sorry," he murmured.

"My fault," she said, taking what blame there was. Collecting herself, she cleared her throat, hoping she hadn't turned a shade of red as a wave of embarrassment ebbed through her. Trying to draw attention from the fact that she had been right in his way in the hope that he *would* kiss her again, she said, "You're doing a nice job, by the way."

He grinned. "I can hit a nail with the best of them." And then he asked, "This your idea, by the way?"

"The Fourth of July?" she deadpanned. "No, I think a bunch of guys in powdered wigs started it a couple hundred years ago—but I might be wrong."

Bringing the ladder over to the next post, he tried to stabilize it again. "No, I mean the celebration, wise guy."

"That was originally Dad's idea," she explained. Positioning herself on the other side of the ladder, she helped him find the most level area. "He wanted to do something for the guests who were staying here at that time of year. We've held a Fourth of July celebration here for as long as I can remember," she said, thinking back over the years. "I just took over a few years ago because, well, Dad is a wonderful man but he's not much at innovation, or sparkle."

He paused on the second rung to look at her. "Sparkle?"

"You have to have sparkle at an event. Otherwise, what's the point?"

"And you bring the sparkle." He could well believe that. She seemed to do it every time she entered a room. She certainly did it whenever she entered his room, or what was temporarily his room, he silently corrected, climbing farther up the ladder until he was level with the row of streamers.

"I find the sparkle to bring to it," she told him. "Dad started out by putting me in charge of finding the fireworks—he could never find the ones that really lit up the sky. My first year in college, I knew these people on campus who could get some great fireworks so I bought some to bring to Dad. Little by little, he gave me more responsibility and along the way, I found I had a knack for planning events."

Shading her eyes, she looked up at Mike. Memories from the past came flooding in, mingling with the memory being created right now. The one that featured him.

A sadness suddenly took hold of her. She struggled out of its grip. "Although this might be my last one," she told Mike.

"You quitting the event planning business?" he asked her, hammering in the last nail on the post.

She didn't answer his question directly. Instead, she said, "I was thinking of going to New York."

"For a visit?" he asked, then looked down at her. "Or permanently?"

"Haven't made up my mind yet." She thought she had. She'd been leaning toward a move—and then he'd turned up and the game board suddenly changed, causing her to reevaluate everything. "I paint," she explained.

He climbed down the ladder again and looked at her. "I know."

Stevi stared at him. She'd never mentioned anything and she doubted if anyone else had. There were times she was certain no one took her dedication seriously.

"How—"

"The paintings on your bedroom walls," he said. "Also in the reception area and the dining room. Your signature is in the corner on all of them."

"You noticed them?" Most men didn't pay attention to details like that. They saw a room in its entirety, not the various things that went into creating that room.

"Hard not to. They're very good." She might not be an artist who broke the rules, but in his estimation she definitely had talent.

"Thank you," she murmured, feeling color begin to creep up along her neck again. She tried to turn away so he wouldn't notice, but that would be even more noticeable, she thought.

He'd made her uncomfortable, Mike realized, and changed the subject. "So, about the Fourth of July."

Relieved to be back on neutral ground, Stevi asked, "What about it?"

"Is this celebration just for the guests at the inn, or do a lot of other people attend, as well?" He tried to sound nonchalant as he asked the question, but he had a reason for trying to find out just who would be on the grounds.

Because she could feel that she was still blushing, Stevi busied herself with preparing the lanterns that were to be hung next.

"Mostly it's for the guests, but some of Dad's friends drop by, as well—which is a bigger group than it might sound. Dad likes to be on good terms with everyone. That's why you're liable to see some local firefighters and members of the police department drifting around the back lawn, as well.

"They stop by as friends," she clarified, "not in their professional capacity." She paused for a moment, unaware of the impact that her words had just had, then asked, "You'll come, won't you?"

Served him right, he thought. Served him right for becoming lax and forgetting just who and what he was. He couldn't let his guard down even for a minute, and he had. He couldn't allow them to pay for his error in judgment.

"I don't know," he answered guardedly. "I might be gone by then."

"But it's only a week away," she reminded him. She didn't want to sound as if she was trying to make him stay—but she really was. If he had no hard-and-fast plans, why would he feel that he might just take off before the week was out? Was it something she'd said? For the life of her, nothing came to mind.

"I know," he said carefully, progressing to another post and climbing up again, "but I feel like I've overstayed my welcome."

"Why would you think that?" she asked. "Has anyone said anything to you?" That would be the only reason for his sudden change of heart, she thought. Otherwise, his abrupt shift made no sense—it didn't anyway, she told herself.

He didn't want her focusing on this too closely, just as he didn't want to place her—or her family—in any sort of danger. And associating with him might very well do that if the wrong person saw him with the Romans.

"No," he told her as casually as possible, "but you know that old saying about guests and fish, after a certain amount of time, they start to smell."

"The only thing you have in common with a fish is that at one point, you were both in the water. Stay long enough for the party," she coaxed, even though doing so went against everything she had told herself previously. "There's no reason for you to leave before then. Cris goes all out preparing the food, and this year's fireworks promise to be the best yet. After it's all over, you can go," she told him, then added what she hoped was the winning argument. "Dad would be very disappointed if you left before the celebration."

He liked the man, but couldn't see that his presence mattered to the inn owner one way or another. "What difference could it make to him?"

There was something in his tone that

made her look at him in disbelief. Didn't he understand? "My dad's taken a liking to you, Mike."

"Your father likes everyone," he pointed out. She'd just said so herself.

"Yes, but there are different degrees of that," she insisted. She sensed his sudden restlessness. It was almost as if they were back to square one, the way he had been that first day he came to and tried to leave her room on his own power. He was running from something. She had no idea what, only that whatever it was, if he stayed here, he'd be all right. "Dad feels as if he's given you a safe harbor here at Ladera."

The funny thing was, he had, Mike thought. This past month that he had spent here had been the least troubled, the most tranquil and the happiest days that he could remember spending in any one place.

Ever.

Which was why he knew he had to leave soon. If her father had invited members of the local police department to drop by, then the safest thing he could do for all of them was to disappear before the party. Because there was an outside chance that he might be seen by or encounter one of the people who had been on that cabin cruiser that night he'd had to suddenly dive into the water—or be fatally cut down on deck.

But he couldn't say that to Stevi.

For one thing, it would only be his word against the word of someone her father most likely trusted and in all probability might have even grown up with. He had discovered the other day that Richard Roman was a native to the area.

For another, at least one or two of the members of the police department obviously had found a way to peacefully co-exist with the drug trade by turning a blind eye to it, or keeping it hidden from the local citizens. It had to be something along those lines because, although he didn't trust very readily, he trusted Richard not to be the type to either be involved in the drug trade or to condone anyone else being involved in it.

Although it wasn't his usual method of operation, this time he wanted to withdraw from the scene before his presence here brought consequences with it—and brought down a delicately constructed balance maintained by good and evil in the town of Ladera.

But if he argued about remaining with Stevi, it might raise her suspicions about his own motives. The best thing to do, he decided, was to pretend that he'd changed his mind.

"Okay," he said, climbing down the ladder again. "You talked me into it."

"You'll stay for the celebration?" Stevi asked uncertainly. He'd changed his mind awfully quickly, she thought.

"I'll stay," he replied, because lying was easier than arguing.

He hadn't expected Stevi to throw her arms around him in response to his words. Hadn't expected that rush of sudden emotion that her impulsive movement released within him.

Hadn't expected to have his own arms tighten around her in what was a purely automatic response. As for her brushing her lips against his, that had come up out of left field and instantly drew another automatic response from him, one that had him kissing her back.

The kiss began by mimicking hers and then went off on a tangent of its own, one that imprinted itself on not just his soul, but, he later discovered, on hers.

And it came very close to almost sealing his fate, as well.

CHAPTER FIFTEEN

HE WAS LOSING his edge.

All these years, both the time that he'd
spent in the various foster homes he was
sent to and then the time he had spent
in the field, working undercover, he had
honed his senses until he was keenly
aware of his surroundings. Not just for a
number of hours or once in a while, not
even most of the time, but *all* the time.

He was alert during his waking hours
and even in his sleep because he had
trained himself to sleep lightly with the
proverbial one eye open.

When he'd been in foster homes, it was
done out of a sense of self-preservation.
He'd learned early in the game that there
was no one to look out for him but him.
What few possessions he had could be

easily taken from him if he so much as blinked.

So he didn't blink. He remained vigilant, sacrificing bits and pieces of his humanity as he did so.

Then, when he was out on his own, the field he chose, literally making himself into a chameleon, required the same intense vigilance he'd executed while growing up. It became even more so because this time, if he lowered his guard, it wasn't just his possessions that he stood to lose, but his very life.

Mike had approached staying here, at the inn as a "guest" of the Roman family, the same way: with keen, watchful vigilance. But Stevi and her family had managed to get to him the way criminals never had.

They'd played dirty, he thought wryly. They'd gotten to him by using kindness, by trusting him. Gotten to him in such a way that those razor-sharp senses of his had actually failed him.

They'd all but gone dormant.

He'd never been so keenly aware of that than this morning, when he failed to hear Silvio walk up behind him until the gardener spoke.

"They are good people, the Romans," the low, gravelly voice testified.

Mike swung around, his hands raised to strike. At the last moment he realized that the person standing behind him was Silvio, who, a second away from being struck across the throat, appeared amazingly calm.

The gardener's expression was somber, his eyes, unreadable.

"Sorry," Mike apologized, trying to bury the seriousness of his reaction with an embarrassed shrug. "I didn't hear you come up behind me."

Silvio nodded. Considering that he was very close to his sixth decade, he had an incredible head of dark hair. "And for a man who lives mainly by his reflexes, you find that troubling."

Mike could feel the other man's eyes

all but probing his mind. "I guess I'm a little jumpy," he said by way of an excuse.

Silvio's expression said he knew better. "A man like you does not get jumpy."

There were no two ways about it, Mike thought. Silvio was on a different wavelength than the Romans. The man had obviously come from a different background than the family.

He squared his shoulders as he tried to dismiss the gardener's preconceived notions about him.

"You have no idea what I'm like," he told Silvio.

Silvio's dark, penetrating eyes never left his. "I was a man like you once," he countered. "Always looking over my shoulder, never knowing whom to trust. Being loyal to what I believed in, but never knowing if the people who were with me one day would turn on me the next." He paused, allowing the description to register. "Death came for me several times and always went away empty-handed. Does that sound familiar to you?"

Mike didn't bother responding to the question. They both knew the answer to that. Instead, he asked the gardener, "What changed?"

Silvio leaned on the rake he was holding and looked around the grounds for a moment. Over the years, he had had a hand in renovating almost all the inn's landscaping. This was as much his now as it was Richard Roman's.

"I came here," he replied simply. "Not by my design. By accident—I thought," he added quietly. "Mr. Richard gave me a place to stay and asked for nothing in return. Asked no questions, only listened."

This revelation, coming for apparently no reason, made no sense to Mike. Was something about to happen? "Why are you telling me this now?"

"Because it was something I thought you needed to know." The reply was enigmatic and only served to confuse him further.

Mike shook his head. "Are you telling me to go or to stay?"

"Neither. That is a decision only you can make. No one can make it for you."

For the first time since the gardener had come up behind him, Mike took a long, hard look around the surrounding general area. Without realizing it, he had walked in on a work in progress. Silvio was apparently in the middle of fertilizing a section of the garden.

"Need any help out here?" he asked.

Silvio considered the offer the way he did everything. Carefully, giving no clues as to his feelings about the matter.

"I have several bags of fertilizer on the truck," he said matter-of-factly.

"How many are you going to use today?" Mike asked.

"All of them."

Mike nodded. A deal had been struck in his estimation.

Words weren't necessary.

MAYBE HE WAS coming around and changing his mind, Stevi thought, standing off to one side and watching the two men interact. Maybe Silvio was telling him how staying on at the inn was tantamount to beginning a new life, something she got the feeling Mike wanted, not to mention needed.

Nobody knew Silvio's full story. The only thing she and her sisters were certain of was that the man hadn't always been a gardener. Her dad had said he'd been a doctor in Argentina.

Because of what she felt was an air of mystery around the man, when she'd been younger, she'd envisioned Silvio as being an enforcer before he had come to stay with them. Seeing his medical skills in action recently put an entirely different focus on his past.

Blessed with more than her share of curiosity, Stevi had still made her peace with the idea that she was never going to know Silvio's full story. He had a right to his secrets.

But not knowing Mike's story was a whole different matter. Though she hadn't said anything to anyone, she wanted to know everything there was to know about this man.

Initially, there had been just idle curiosity motivating her, but she'd been willing to let it ride. Now, however, things were different.

Now she was in love with him.

Never having experienced the emotion beyond the puppy-love stage, she was still certain she knew love when she fell into it—and she had, headfirst. And although she'd heard that along with love came respecting the other person's boundaries, in this case she didn't know what those boundaries were and so she was desperately trying to test them.

In effect, she wanted to know every single inch, every single nuance, every single fact there was to know about the man, about his past and about what paths he'd taken that brought him to her shores—literally.

She had no idea how to find out any of this and she instinctively knew that prying into his life wouldn't go over too well.

Moreover, she couldn't shake the feeling that when he talked about leaving, it wasn't just talk. He was serious and about several days—if that much—away from walking out of her life.

She had to find a way to make him want to stay.

"YOU COULD OFFER him a job," she told her father. She'd turned to him as her first avenue of appeal in her quest to get Mike to remain at the inn. "Like you did to Silvio and Dorothy—and Jorge," she threw in for good measure.

"Jorge was already looking for a job when he came to me," her father pointed out. He leaned back in his chair, unconsciously steepling his fingers as he thought. "As for the other two, I told each of them that they had a job here for as long as they felt like staying."

"Okay." Stevi nodded, waiting for her father to say "but."

She didn't have a long wait.

"I offered Mike a job when he came to

me asking for some way to repay me for letting him stay here at the inn."

She realized she was holding her breath as she asked, "And?"

The memory was still very fresh in his mind. "And Mike said he was just looking for some kind of temporary work, nothing permanent."

"Temporary turns into permanent sometimes," she pointed out. There was no missing the hopeful note in her voice.

"True, but prodding doesn't work in this case. We'll just have to wait and see how it goes. Mike *does* know that he's welcome to stay here for as long as he needs to." He looked at his daughter for a long moment, studying her closely. "The problem is that his definition of 'needs to' could be totally different from ours." Richard smiled broadly at his daughter. "Cheer up, honey. My mother used to say that if something was meant to be, it would be."

"It can be a lot easier if you make it be," she told her father. When he looked at her quizzically, waiting for her to elaborate, she said, "If you ask him to stay on, he wouldn't turn you down."

"I can't make him stay if he doesn't want to, Stevi. Besides," he said, looking at her knowingly, "I don't think I'm the deciding factor in his ultimate decision whether to go or to remain."

The way her father was looking at her led her to only one conclusion. "You think it's me?" she asked incredulously.

He knew it was her. "I've seen the way he looks at you when he thinks no one else is watching. I'd say that you figure very prominently into Mike's decision about his future."

She sighed, feeling as if she was trying to swim upstream and the current was relentlessly pushing her back. "You're telling me he's leaving because of me?"

Richard looked at her, apparently puzzled. "He hasn't said anything to me about leaving."

Stevi blew out a breath, wishing she was as confident about this as her father was. But she really doubted she'd gotten her signals crossed.

"Mike was helping me hang the streamers and the lanterns for the celebration and I asked him if he was going to attend the party. He didn't think he'd be here by then."

She knew she shouldn't allow the note of desperation to enter her voice but it did anyway. "Dad, it's only a few days away." She bit her lower lip.

"Why don't you focus on the time you have?" her father suggested kindly. "Who knows? Maybe Mike'll wind up changing his mind, or delaying his so-called departure date—and then all this agonizing you're going through would have been for no reason."

Stevi read between the lines. It wasn't hard. She knew her father. "So you won't talk to him?"

"Honey, you can't pressure anyone into doing something they don't want to. A lot of times, having a talk with someone winds up getting the exact opposite reaction."

"I'll try to remember that the next time Alex starts trying to order me around," Stevi said, trying her best to look as cheerful as she knew her father wanted her to be. It wasn't easy.

"By the way," he segued into a question he'd been meaning to ask, "speaking of job offers, have you given my offer any more thought?"

Her father's proposition was never very far from her mind. "You mean your putting me on salary as the inn's event planner?"

He smiled as he nodded. "That's what I mean."

"I'm still thinking about it," Stevi told him. She slanted a glance in his direction. "Maybe if Mike was staying on, I'd be more inclined to stay, too."

He assumed she wasn't really being serious—but just in case she was, Richard told her, "Blackmail does not suit you, Stevi. I didn't raise you that way."

But she had a reminder of her own to bring up. "But you *did* raise me to be resourceful, remember?"

He laughed and shook his head. "You know, you really should have become a lawyer, Stevi. You have a knack for twisting things around until they come out to your advantage. Clients like that when you do it in their favor."

"If only it worked on my father, as well," she said brightly, batting her eyelashes at him in an exaggerated fashion, lest he took her seriously.

"Go." Her father laughed, pointing toward his door. "Some of us have work to do. Come to think of it, all of us do. The Fourth is closer than you might think."

That, she thought, leaving his office and closing the door behind her, was exactly what she was acutely aware of.

MIKE WAS STILL helping Silvio with the last of the bags of fertilizer they had brought off the truck when she came looking for him.

"Are you and your strong back available to me later on, or does Silvio have dibs on you for the rest of the afternoon?" she asked innocently, looking from Mike to the gardener.

"You've come just at the right time, Miss Stevi," Silvio told her. "I am finished with him if you want him."

Oh, gosh, do I ever, she caught herself thinking even as she remembered to paste a smile on her lips.

"I guess that answers your question," Mike said, stripping off the thick work gloves Silvio must have loaned him when he'd started the job. He held them out to the gardener. "Thanks."

Silvio nodded, sticking them in his back pocket. He went about his work without a word—but Stevi had the feeling that the man was watching them as they walked away and continued to watch them until they disappeared around the side of the inn.

"I'm surprised Silvio accepted your

help," she said once they were out of what she assumed was the gardener's earshot.

"Why's that?" Because of his upbringing, or more accurately, the lack thereof, he had become a jack-of-all-trades, except that he tried to be as good in whatever endeavor he was currently working as he possibly could.

"Because Silvio's the type who likes to work alone and I think he also likes to appear as if he doesn't need anyone's help." Amusement curved the corners of her mouth, but only fleetingly as she said, "I guess he never bought into John Donne's 'no man is an island' theory. That's a—"

"A poem, yes, I know," he said, nodding.

"You took poetry?" she asked incredulously. She couldn't see someone like Mike signing up for a poetry class. He would have to be taken in, kicking and screaming.

"I *read* poetry on my own," he corrected her. "Worked in a bookstore for a while. Did a lot of reading on my breaks and during lunch."

The revelation surprised her. She couldn't picture him reading poetry willingly. And from what he hadn't said, she surmised that he hadn't gone to college.

She had to think before she spoke, Stevi thought, upbraiding herself. She hadn't wanted to hurt his feelings for the world.

"You know, they say that life's the best college, the best teacher anyone could have," she told him.

He knew what she was doing. She was trying to make him feel better about the path he'd taken.

He was surprised that this touched him. But it did.

"'They' say a lot of things," he pointed out. "Now, what is it you need help with?"

Finding a way to get you to stay.

Out loud Stevi said, "I need you to help me move a few things out onto the back lawn. They're all right this way." She gestured toward the area he'd helped her decorate the other day. "Follow me."

I only wish I could. The thought tele-graphed itself through his mind before he could stop it.

CHAPTER SIXTEEN

"Do you remember yet?"

"Excuse me?" Mike looked up at her, caught off guard by the out-of-the-blue question.

They had been working together for a good part of the afternoon, occasionally being interrupted by guests wanting to know details about the inn's Fourth of July celebration. Despite that, they'd accomplished a great deal.

Struggling, they'd managed to erect a long, rectangular red, white and blue awning, which would shelter the food on the buffet table. For the most part, it was to shade the guests and the food from the sun, although there had been talk of the possibility of rain on the big day, anywhere between ten to twenty percent chance, depending on which news station Stevi tuned to. She'd rented the awning as a precaution, just in case twenty percent turned out to be a reality.

The final decorations were hung up and all in place. The big day was still three days off, but Stevi, he had discovered, didn't like leaving things to the last minute. It made her nervous, she'd told him.

The only thing that needed to be done on the actual day, besides the cooking, would be to bring out the tables and chairs for those who preferred to sit while they ate.

After working for several hours straight, Stevi had suggested that they break for an early dinner. Rather than eat in the dining area, because the weather was as perfect as it got in San Diego County—a moderate, comfortable temperature accompanied by a soft summer breeze—she'd suggested that they avail themselves of the party area and eat outside.

Mike had set up one of the small, round tables and brought out two folding chairs.

They brought their plates of, appropriately enough, fried chicken outside and enjoyed the peaceful solitude.

That was when Stevi had asked him whether he remembered anything yet.

The question, when he replayed it in his head and realized what she was asking, brought reality sharply back into focus. Stalling for time didn't really help him come up with an answer. He had no pat story for her.

Moreover, he found himself not wanting to offer her a pat story.

He wanted, instead, to be honest with her even though he knew he couldn't be. For a number of reasons, both professional and personal.

"Do you remember anything yet?" she pressed. She'd hoped that by now his recovery would be nearly complete, and he'd be able to recall the memories that had eluded him. She tried to make her reason for asking as innocuous sounding as possible because she didn't want him to feel as if she was pushing—even though, technically, she was. "It's been a month and I was just wondering if anything's jostled your memory yet."

"You're asking me if I remember who shot me," he said bluntly.

"Actually, I'm asking not just that but if you remember anything at all," she stressed. "Where you come from, who you are, what you did for a living before you did an imitation of a seashell and washed up on the beach."

"Is that important to you?" he asked, wanting to know if, for some miraculous reason, things worked themselves out, if he could remain here like Dorothy and Silvio before him, would she be satisfied with the man he was trying to be or did she need to know about the man he'd been?

And if it was the latter, would she accept him or find him lacking and send him away? Would she focus on the heroics in his life, or at bottom, would she just see the foster kid nobody wanted and ask him to go away?

"I'm just curious," Stevi said. "I always have been. I always need to know how a book ends. It's the same with secrets," she said, lowering her voice. "I *have* to know. I wouldn't pass it on, wouldn't tell a soul, but I just need to know." She flashed a smile at him. "Working for the FBI or the CIA would probably drive me crazy."

He did a double take. Why had she mentioned those organizations? Did she suspect? Or was that just an off-the-cuff remark?

"Sometimes secrets are best kept just that—secret," he told her quietly.

Her eyes met his and she looked at him for a long, drawn-out moment before she said, "Then you don't remember anything."

"What I remember," he said in the same low, calm voice as he reached for her hand, "is opening my eyes and seeing this blonde, blue-eyed vision looking down at me, and thinking that I was either dreaming or had died and reached the threshold of heaven. As far as I'm concerned, everything that came before then was part of another lifetime, another reality. Mine started a month ago, with the sand beneath my back and your face blocking out the sun."

She could feel her heart hammering even as she silently told herself not to get carried away. There could be a number of ways to interpret his words. Still, she needed to put the question to him.

"Does that mean you've decided to stay?" she asked uncertainly.

Mike was saying everything she wanted to hear, but something within her doubted that it was the truth. It wasn't that she thought he was deliberately lying; she just had the feeling that this was his way of trying to spare her pain.

It was as if he'd looked into her heart, seen his name written there and knew what she was feeling for him. Knew that leaving her would be really upsetting for her. So, while he was still here, he was telling her what she wanted to hear.

With all her heart, Stevi wished she could believe him.

What she *could* believe was that he was trying to be kind to her. That he cared about her in some small way and that, she told herself, was going to have to be enough for her.

Ha!

As if....

"I can't very well desert you in the middle of all these preparations. You still need someone to set up the tables and chairs on the Fourth, right?" Mike reminded her.

"I'm also going to need help breaking everything down after the celebration's over—most likely that will be the day after the Fourth," she amended, "since the fireworks are going to be around eight-thirty, or as soon as it's dark. A couple of our guests brought their young children with them and I don't want them being up very late—although if they turn out to be anything like Ricky," she said, "they'll be putting their parents to bed while they're still raring to go."

Mike shook his head. "I didn't know that there were all these logistics involved in throwing what's supposed to be just a simple celebration."

"That's why these days they refer to it as event planning. Because of all the details involved, all the different people who might be attending, a great deal of planning goes into throwing almost any kind of party."

Had she taken his offhand comment as an insult? "I didn't mean to make it sound as if I was belittling what you do—" he said, thinking that if he'd put his foot in his mouth, he needed to correct that right away.

He almost looked flustered, she thought, amused at his reaction. He looked his most adorable when he was being his most human, rather than the strong, silent type—although that, too, had its appeal.

Face it, Stevi, you've got it bad.

"No offense taken," she assured him. "That's why they have event planners, because most people don't think of all the contingencies that might come into play. I don't, either," she confessed in case he thought she was bragging that she could think of *everything,* "but I am better than most people at remembering the minutia." He was smiling. Why? "What?" she asked, raising her eyebrows.

"Your eyes dance when you talk about what you do," he observed.

"No, they don't," she protested with a laugh.

Event planning wasn't her passion. This job was a temporary sidebar, a place filler, just something she was doing at the moment until she found her true calling, the really important thing that she could dedicate herself to accomplishing. Using balloons to underscore themes did not fit into that category.

"I beg to differ," Mike said, interrupting. "I'm on the other side of those eyes, so I'd know. You can't see them the way I can. There's no shame in enjoying your work. It *is* important in its own way."

Now he was pandering to her. "Yeah, right."

Mike wouldn't be dissuaded. "You create memories for people."

Anything she was going to add to her dismissal of her work vanished. She looked at him in surprise. "What a lovely thing to say."

Mike shrugged, turning his attention to the soft drink in his glass as he took a sip. "Yeah, that's me, the guy who says lovely things."

"You do," she insisted. "What you say makes a person feel special." She paused, then decided she had nothing to lose by speaking up and perhaps something to gain. "You made me feel special."

Surprised, Mike raised his eyes to hers. "Ditto," he whispered after a moment.

Ditto.

Not exactly one of the most romantic words in the English language, Stevi thought, but she'd take it because the sentiment behind that word *was* romantic, at least in her eyes, and that, she realized, was very, very important to her.

"Thank you," she murmured.

Mike shrugged again, meaning to shrug off her thanks and anything else that went with it. Sentiment—any other emotion other than anger, he supposed—made him uncomfortable.

He only understood anger because he'd grown up with it, a great deal of it.

Stevi and her family were ruining him, he thought, not for the first time. They were making him think things he had no business thinking. Feeling things he had no right to feel. Yearning for what was completely out of his reach.

Moreover, for them to continue having the life they had, he needed to leave so that nothing and no one could threaten it or disrupt it.

But he didn't want her thinking he'd just turned his back and walked away. Didn't want her thinking that he'd just used her for his own ends because he needed a place to heal and someone to tend to his wounds, the way she had insisted on doing.

Because she'd given him so much, given him something to dream about, no matter how unattainable, he wanted to give her something in return.

A piece of himself because he had nothing else to offer.

"I grew up in the system," he reminded her abruptly. "Foster care. I never knew my parents. Didn't know if they died or just couldn't be bothered and gave me up."

Stunned both at what she was hearing and that he was actually telling her something like this, Stevi stared at him. More than anything she wanted to comfort him, but she knew that he would see it as pity and would withdraw from her, his pride wounded.

So she kept her silence and let him talk. That was all that she could do for him.

"The parents I did get to know didn't give a damn about me one way or another. Even the best of them—and I use the term loosely—were in it for the monthly check from social services.

"The second I aged out, I was gone."

The story could stop here and his secret would still remain safe. She'd have her glimpse into his life and he would still retain the anonymity that was the hallmark of his existence. But that was only half of who he was and he wanted to let her see the other side of him.

"My first job was at a mom-and-pop store. Guy who owned it, Lee, was decent enough. He didn't work me too hard and gave me the day-old foodstuffs to take home with me.

"One night, he and I were closing up and these two hoods came in and tried to rob him. They weren't happy that there wasn't much in the register so they started beating him. I guess something just snapped inside me. I got the drop on them and suddenly I was the one doing the beating. When it was over, they were the ones on the floor.

"The cop who was first on the scene

took my statement. Instead of hauling me in, he asked if I'd ever thought about becoming a cop myself. A couple of days later, I went down to the precinct to see him. He gave me some brochures, introduced me to a couple people. I knew what my destiny was...." Mike's voice trailed off as he shrugged, letting her fill in the blanks for herself.

Stevi's eyes widened. "You're a policeman?" she asked.

Since he'd come this far, he decided to give her the more accurate description of what he did. "I was, before I became an undercover DEA agent."

It wasn't hard for her to put the rest together. "You were shot while you were on the job." It wasn't a question, it was a statement.

After a moment, he inclined his head and said, "Something like that."

She knew she couldn't ask for any details because he wouldn't be able to tell her. But there was one thing she could ask. "Isn't there someone you should be reporting this to?"

His smile was warm, she thought, and for the first time, almost boyish. "I am. You."

"I mean someone official." He didn't answer. "So you've decided to take a break, is that it?"

It was as good an explanation as any, he supposed. And maybe even accurate to an extent. Since he didn't know the good guys from the bad guys without a scorecard, he'd just stepped back from everything until he could gain some perspective about what mattered.

His decision not to get in contact with anyone to let them know he was alive was because just before he'd been shot he'd caught a glimpse of Larry Crenshaw, one of the main men involved in the drug smuggling ring, on this side of the border. From the local police department. Mike had a feeling the guy had been the one to blow his cover.

What he didn't have a clue about was

how many more people had a foot in both worlds. If he told the wrong person about this discovery—and that person was also involved, he'd be signing his own death warrant. At the moment, everyone who'd been on that cruiser thought he was dead and he'd decided to make use of that by just disappearing altogether.

He'd thought, for a little while, that the inn was the perfect place where he could disappear. After all, Silvio had and the man hadn't exactly been a choirboy before he landed on Richard Roman's doorstep.

But now he knew he'd just been fooling himself. This was far too visible a place to "disappear." The people on that cruiser, the one or ones from this area, were bound to see him sooner or later and then he really would be dead.

Which, when he came down to it, wasn't such a big deal one way or the other. Part of him had been dead a long time anyway. But the fact that harm might come to any of these good people who had taken him in was something he couldn't live with, couldn't accept. If anything happened to any of them, especially Stevi, he'd never forgive himself. He had to disappear rather than risk something like that ever possibly happening.

"You could call it a break," he agreed. "A permanent one. I realized there didn't seem to be much of a purpose in fighting. The bad guys just keep coming," he told her. "You kill one, another comes to take his place. And another, and another."

"But if you don't take them off the street, there's that many more who are *on* the street, that many more who can hurt people. Who can hurt children," Stevi emphasized.

He looked at her, trying to fathom what she was saying. "Are you telling me you think I should go back into the ranks?"

"Doesn't matter what I think," she said, placing her hand over his. "And what I'm telling you to do is to follow your conscience."

He laughed shortly. "Sorry, my conscience was the first casualty."

She couldn't believe that. Didn't believe that. "No, it wasn't. You're a good man, Mike. I can tell."

He shrugged, looking away. "If that's what you want to believe, I can't stop you, but you're wrong. I'm not." He'd lost track of who he was, what he was, a long time ago.

"Maybe I'm wrong about other things—my sisters will be happy to give you a long list, verbal and otherwise, of my misjudgments and mistakes—but I'm not wrong about this. I'm definitely not wrong about this."

CHAPTER SEVENTEEN

"So, DO YOU think that our Stevi is going to decide not to go to New York after all and stay put here instead?"

Alex put the question to Cris as she stood in the kitchen, sipping a rather large cup of freshly brewed vanilla chai tea. The break in her regular routine was her one concession to both her doctor's orders and Wyatt's pleas to take things a little easier for a while.

As she spoke, she held the cup in both hands, letting its warmth radiate out to her palms.

Despite the fact that it was summer, there was a chill in her bones that Alex couldn't quite get rid of. She chalked it up to being pregnant and her hormones going wild.

A little like the rest of her, she supposed.

"You know our Stevi," Cris replied, her attention focused, for the most part, on the twenty-five miniature apple-cinnamon pies she was preparing for dinner. "Nothing's ever definite with her until after it's happened."

Her restlessness kicked into high gear despite the tea, Alex had drifted over to the window, which afforded a limited view of the lawn out back and the ocean beyond it.

"Oh, I think it's happened already," Alex said, looking out the window. Specifically, she was looking at her sister sharing a meal with the man she had rescued a month ago.

Stevi and Mike looked good together, she thought. Maybe destiny had taken things into its own hands.

Cris glanced up and saw where her sister was looking. Inasmuch as Stevi had come in about twenty minutes ago, ask-

ing for two plates of food, it wasn't difficult for her to put two and two together.

"You mean Mike?" she asked.

"No, I mean Brad Pitt," Alex answered
impatiently as she looked at Cris. "I heard
he's leaving Angelina and coming here to
ask Stevi to marry him. Of course I mean
Mike." Alex looked back out the window.
Their body language said a lot. They were
into each other even if they didn't know it.
"Stevi's like a whole different person ever
since she found Mike on the beach and
took him on as her own personal project."

Cris stopped rolling out another ball of
dough, her attention diverted by something she heard in her sister's voice.

"You think they might…?"

"Yes, I think they 'might,'" Alex replied. "Why? You disapprove?"

A lock of Cris's hair came loose from
the clip she used to keep it pulled back
and she moved it out of her eye with the
back of her wrist.

"Disapprove?" she echoed incredulously. "No, of course not. I think he's a

really nice guy and Stevi seems happier around him than she's been in a long time. It's just that…"

Why did Cris insist on doing that? On letting her voice trail off like that? It drove her crazy. But then, since she'd become pregnant, *so* many things drove her crazy. "That what?" Alex asked impatiently.

"It's just that I wish we knew more about him," Cris said.

Alex laughed shortly. The lack of information about the newcomer really didn't bother her at this point. The inn served as a safe haven for people from time to time. It had been that way for as far back as she could remember.

"How much did we know about Dorothy or Silvio when Dad took them in?" Alex pointed out. "They both turned out to be really good for the inn—and for our family." There had been other people as well, but they had, for the most part, moved on, after staying as long as they could—and a little longer. "Maybe Mike will, too."

"Maybe," Cris agreed, getting back to work. "I guess what I'm trying to say is that I just don't want to see Stevi hurt, that's all."

Abandoning the window, Alex crossed to the steel table where her sister was working.

"And by that you mean what?" she questioned, bending slightly in order to get a better look at Cris's face. "You don't think he's going to stay, do you?"

"I really don't know," Cris answered. "But I get the feeling that he's not all that at peace." And then she shrugged and, in a lighter tone, concluded, "Or maybe it's just me and these hormones."

"Hormones?" Alex echoed with a scoff. "Please, don't get me started on hormones. I had no idea I could run the gamut from high to low and back again in under sixty seconds before. You certainly didn't give me a clue when you found out you were pregnant," she accused, sparing Cris a long, hard look.

Maybe Alex should have taken her cue

from what she had been physically going through at the time, Cris thought. "I was too busy throwing up to say anything to anyone," she pointed out.

"Excuse not accepted," Alex informed her, then glanced at her watch. "Time for me to get back to the desk."

Now that she looked at her, Alex did look a little peaked.

"Why don't you have Dad spell you?" Cris suggested. "I know he wouldn't mind going back to manning the reception desk for a little while, especially if he's doing it so that his pregnant daughter could get some rest."

Alex frowned at the suggestion. It went against everything she believed in. "I am not about to use my condition as an excuse not to do my job, Cris."

Why was everything with Alex an argument, Cris wondered wearily. "I'm not telling you not to do your job. I'm just telling you it's okay to lighten up a little once in a while."

Alex glared at her. "Says the woman

who practically delivered in the kitchen, cooking."

"I got to the hospital in time."

Alex laughed. "Just barely and only because it was the break between lunch and dinner. In between contractions you were worried that there wasn't enough consommé on hand for Dorothy to make beef stroganoff for the guests the way the menu promised."

Cris knew she couldn't very well claim that it didn't happen that way since it did. "I guess being obsessed runs in the family," she replied.

"I'll say. I barely survived Stevi being in charge of my wedding."

"Our wedding," Cris corrected automatically. Taking a tablespoon full of sugar, she drizzled it across the tops of the pie crusts.

"It didn't become 'our' until the last minute," Alex reminded her. "You had barely an hour. I had over a month of her bossing me around."

Cris grinned. Turning from the worktable, she regarded her older sister. "How did it feel being on the receiving end for a change?"

Alex pressed her lips together. "I think I'd better get back to the reception desk before this winds up being an argument."

Cris feigned surprise and laid her wrist to her forehead, melodramatically. "You wouldn't want to upset a pregnant woman now, would you?"

"I already have," Alex retorted as she left the kitchen. "Me."

"Lots of luck, Alex's son or daughter," Cris murmured under her breath. "Your mom's a pistol, but you can always come and cry on Aunt Cris's shoulder anytime."

Smiling at the prospect, Cris went on making miniature pies.

"Can I help?"

The high-pitched, inquisitive voice came from directly behind him—where he had assumed, until just now, that Stevi was standing.

Then he remembered that Stevi had said

something about going to scrounge up more nails, so he realized that it couldn't be her asking the question.

Besides, Stevi's voice was far more melodic and not that high-pitched.

Mike turned to find Stevi's nephew standing behind him, his head cocked to one side, his eyes opened wide to take in everything that was being done.

Ricky was here by himself.

"Isn't there supposed to be somebody with you?" Mike asked.

As far as he had observed since he'd been here, the energetic boy was never alone. There was always an adult just a few steps away, supervising him because he was so very energetic. But when Mike scanned the immediate area again, he didn't see either of the boy's parents, his doting aunts, uncle or grandfather anywhere in the vicinity.

Apparently, for now, it was just the boy. And him.

Children made him uncomfortable. He had no idea what to do with them or how to communicate with them for that matter. As far as any dealings with them went, they seemed to be a whole breed apart to him, like tiny alien beings.

During his own childhood he'd never been able to really relate to or interact with any of the kids he found himself thrown in with. Part of the problem arose from the fact that he was never around any other child long enough to form a relationship. So he became a loner. In the long run, it was easier that way.

"Grandpa's supposed to be minding me," Ricky volunteered.

Mike scanned the area a third time. Except for the two guests strolling away from the inn in the distance, there was no one else around and definitely no sign of the boy's grandfather.

"Where is he?" Mike asked.

"In his office. Talking to somebody." Ricky shrugged his small, slender shoulders. "It was boring so I came outside. I heard you hammering. Can I help hammer?" he asked again. "I like to hammer things."

"I just bet you do," Mike murmured more to himself than the boy.

As if to try to convince him to hand over the tool under discussion, Ricky added, "Daddy says I'm good at it. He's not my real daddy but he's nice so it's okay. My real daddy's dead."

Mike almost dropped his hammer at the little guy's sad revelation. He was at a loss how to respond to that news. Gripping the handle of the tool more tightly he began to fish for something, anything, to say. "I… It's quite a… I mean, you—"

"He was a soldier."

Mike sucked in a breath. *Harsh.* "At least you knew who your dad was," he muttered under his breath, as he still struggled with what to say to the kid about his huge loss.

"You never met your daddy?" he asked sympathetically.

Did kids that age even *have* sympathy, Mike thought, amazed. He hadn't the vaguest idea what, if anything, went through a child's head. Where was Stevi, anyway? She could talk to the kid. He sure couldn't.

But it was obvious that the boy was waiting for some sort of a response. "No, I never met my father."

"Me, neither," Ricky responded. "Mama said he was killed before I was born, so I couldn't meet him. I guess we're alike, huh? You can borrow my new daddy if you wanna," he offered. "Mama says it's good to share."

Where *was* she? He looked around impatiently again, but he didn't see Stevi. This boy was killing him. "Thanks, kid, but I'm too old for a daddy."

"No, you're not. Mama's old like you and she's got a daddy," he said, proving his point. "Grandpa's her daddy. Would you like to share him instead?"

As if on cue, Richard hurried from the veranda and came down the steps as quickly as he could, heading directly for the boy.

"Oh, thank heaven, there you are, Ricky!" Reaching him, Richard wrapped the boy in a bear hug, relieved beyond words. "You made my heart stop," he cried.

"Is it still stopped?" the boy asked, looking at him curiously.

"No, it's beating again," Richard assured him with a relieved laugh, still holding on to the boy. Ricky was fearless and had already wandered off more than once, despite repeated warnings and entreaties not to.

"That's good," Ricky replied. "But you're squishing me, Grandpa. I can't breathe."

"Sorry." Richard loosened his hold on his grandson. He looked up at Mike. "I got caught up in a conversation with a friend of mine and when I looked around, Ricky was gone." He shook his head. "They move faster than lightning at this age."

"Grandpa was talking to a policeman," Ricky said, stretching out the word. "He had a gun and everything. But he wouldn't let me touch it." He pouted.

"Guns aren't safe to hold," Mike told him gruffly.

Ricky's expression was the personification of innocence as he asked, "Why not?"

"Ricky, don't bother Mike," Richard chided. "You can see that he's busy helping Aunt Stevi decorate for the Fourth of July party."

"They go off," Mike said. "When somebody who isn't familiar with a gun holds it, sometimes the gun goes off. That's dangerous."

There had been an incident in one of the foster homes he had been in. Another boy had gotten into the family's gun cabinet, which had been left unlocked. The girl he'd aimed at hadn't survived the trip to the hospital. The incident had left him with a very healthy respect for weapons, even those that were supposedly unloaded.

He had no idea how to convey that to

Ricky, or how much he could or couldn't tell him.

"Oh," Ricky replied, instantly subdued. "Do people get dead, then?"

He paused, then made a judgment call and said, "Sometimes."

Ricky turned to Richard. "You should tell your friend to throw his gun away, Grandpa. So you don't get dead." He threw his small arms around his grandfather as far as they could reach. "I don't want you dead."

Richard stroked the boy's silky hair. "Don't worry, Ricky. Officer Crenshaw's been a policeman for a long time. He knows how to handle his gun."

Crenshaw.

The name shot like a bullet right into his consciousness.

"This Officer Crenshaw," Mike said in an emotionless voice.

Richard was trying to gently peel his grandson's arms away from the death grip the boy was executing. "Yes, what about him?"

"What's his first name?" Mike asked casually.

"Larry." Curious, Richard looked at him quizzically. "Why?"

"No reason," Mike answered, a shrug accompanying his words. "I knew someone named Crenshaw once. Thought it might be the same person."

"Is it?"

Mike shook his head. "No. The guy I knew was David."

Except that he wasn't. He was Larry. And he didn't actually know him, but what he *did* know was that the man on the cruiser, the local law enforcement officer who he suspected was the one responsible for blowing his cover, that man's name was Larry Crenshaw.

The pieces fell together.

The man, according to Ricky, that Richard had been talking to in his office, the man Richard acknowledged as his friend, was involved in drug trafficking. This same man, he was certain, had seen him take a header off the side of the boat after being shot.

And in addition, in all likelihood, from everything that Stevi and the other members of her family had said to him, Crenshaw was probably going to stop by the celebration at some point.

With his luck, their paths would cross, or the man might see him while he didn't see Crenshaw.

Either way, he was a dead man.

Again.

And this time, Stevi's family might be made to pay, as well.

Any choice to stay he thought he had left was obviously gone. Because even if he lay low and didn't attend the celebration, if this Crenshaw was a friend of Richard's, he was liable to pop up at the inn at any time.

He certainly couldn't stay in his room from here on until he either died or Crenshaw moved. That was impossible as well as ridiculous.

He had no choice, Mike thought darkly. He had to leave and the sooner the better.

That only made sense. He didn't need to wait until the last minute. The only reason to hesitate for even another hour was because it meant that he had another hour left to spend with Stevi.

The thought surprised him.

It wasn't like him.

He'd never gotten attached to a place or a person. Not for as long as he could remember. Attachments were nothing more than heartaches waiting to happen and he wasn't about to be on the receiving end of something like that. It was too painful, too damaging to his self-esteem. He'd learned how to harden himself against attachments.

And yet, despite that, he could feel this yearning to linger, to squeeze out as much time as he could down to the very last second, because he *knew* he was never going to feel like this again.

Never feel anything for anyone again.

This was just a fluke and once he walked out that door, it was over.

Gone.

"Mike—"

He blinked, realizing that while he had gone off on a mental tangent, Richard had been talking to him and whatever he'd said, he was winding up now.

He did his best to replay the words he hadn't been paying attention to and make sense out of what was now being said.

"—since we're talking here, I wanted to ask you to dinner tomorrow night."

Just how much had he missed? "What's tomorrow night?" Mike asked point-blank. The man made it sound as if it was something special.

Richard laughed and said almost shyly, "Fourth of July Eve, if you will. I like to gather the family together for a private meal before all the chaos ensues the next day."

What did that have to do with him? "But I'm not—"

Richard held up one hand. The other was holding on to his grandson's hand.

"Save it. I know what you're going to say. That you're not part of the family. My answer to that is that it takes more than just blood and an ancestry chart to make a family. Say you'll attend. It would mean a lot to me."

"And me!" Ricky piped up, as if he didn't want to be left out and had been quiet, in his estimation, far too long. *"Me!"* he repeated more loudly.

"And me."

Mike turned to see that Stevi had returned, bearing a box of long nails.

If he demurred or tried to talk his way out of it, it would only draw out the discussion to persuade him to attend—and, short of just walking away, he'd lose anyway. He had no avenue open to him but to say yes.

"Well, put that way, how can I say no?" he asked.

Stevi smiled in response, but even so,

she wondered if she was the only one who noticed that Mike *hadn't* actually said yes to her father's invitation.

CHAPTER EIGHTEEN

"You are coming, aren't you?" Stevi asked Mike as soon as her father and Ricky were out of earshot.

He took the nails that she had brought and tucking them into the front pocket of the jeans he had on, he climbed back up the ladder to nail hooks for the remaining lanterns.

"Like I said," he repeated, his back to her, "how could I refuse?"

Holding on to the foot of the ladder, Stevi pointed out, "That's not a yes, Mike, that's just another question."

Hanging up the lantern, he looked down at her. "Well, then, I guess I'd better say yes to set your mind at ease." With that, he climbed down again. There were four lanterns left to hang. He moved the ladder over to the next pole.

"I know that they—that we," she corrected, including herself in the group, "can be a bit difficult to take at times. We might seem as if we come on a little strong—or maybe a lot," she conceded, "depending on what you're used to—"

He paused, his eyes meeting hers. "What I'm used to," he told her, "are people who don't care. Discovering people who do takes a bit of getting used to," he admitted, then smiled at her, "but it's definitely worth it."

She studied him, attempting to read between the lines. "So you're not angry?"

The question appeared to take him aback. "Why would I be angry?"

She inclined her head, trying to phrase this just the right way. "Because it might have sounded as if my father was trying to pressure you into attending his private dinner tomorrow night."

He was surprised at her reasoning, and then shook his head. "By telling me he considers me as part of the family? There're a lot of ways to get on my bad side, Stevi, but that's not one of them," he told her. "I'll be there," he promised.

And he intended to keep that promise— then leave right afterward, when they were all asleep. He wasn't much on goodbyes, couldn't really remember the last time he'd actually said the words and felt anything. But he'd feel something this time, which was why he wasn't going to put himself in the position of having to say them out loud. Slipping out quietly would be far better for everyone concerned.

Especially him.

Because if he had to say goodbye, maybe he wouldn't—and that would ultimately be putting all of them in danger. He couldn't repay their kindness that way, no matter how much he wanted to stay.

She looked at the last three lanterns in the box. They could easily be put up tomorrow. Because of Mike's help, she was comfortably ahead of schedule.

"Listen, I've been ordering you around

for a good part of today. What do you say we just knock off now, enjoy what's left of the evening?" Dusk was beginning to creep in, creating a very romantic ambiance.

That was fine with him, but he was surprised that she was the one suggesting it. "I thought you wanted to finish decorating everything?"

"We've still got tomorrow," Stevi pointed out. Suddenly, adhering obsessively to timetables wasn't all that important anymore. Enjoying the evening with Mike was.

"Yes, we've still got tomorrow," he agreed. And that was all he had, he thought.

About to say something else, Stevi stopped and looked at him. Maybe it was her imagination, but there was something in his voice, a finality, for lack of a better term, that made her very uneasy. It was as if "tomorrow" wasn't one more day, but one *last* day.

"You're looking at me strangely," Mike observed, wondering why. "What?"

"Nothing," Stevi said, shrugging off his question and looking away.

"No, it's definitely something," Mike countered.

He'd never been the type to push personal issues. A person's reason for behaving a certain way was their own business. But there was something in her eyes, something so sad that it touched him and he felt he needed to get to the source of it. Needed to make her stop looking so sad.

Leave it be. The less you let her pull you in, the better it is for both of you. If you connect, leaving's going to be that much harder. Use your head.

He almost laughed at himself. All those thoughts would have carried a lot more weight a couple of weeks ago. But now? Now it was too late. Stevi had already pulled him in. He was *already* entangled with these people. With her family.

With her.

Leaving them was going to be the hardest thing he'd ever done. And probably the most decent.

Shivering, she ran her hands up and down along her arms. "Ever feel a chill? The kind that means someone just jumped over your grave?"

"I've felt a chill," he replied. "But that was usually because the jacket I had on—*if* I had a jacket—was threadbare. And for the record, I don't buy into superstitions," he said. "They're just fairy tales with a creepy angle." He looked at her for a long moment, wishing he could hold her. Knowing how unwise that would be. "If you're chilly, maybe we should go inside."

"No, I'm okay," she protested. She wasn't ready to go inside, to be around other people. She wanted to be with just him. "What I'd like is to take a walk with you on the beach, like we did that night you couldn't sleep."

"If that's what you want," he said gamely. "Sure, why not? Let's go." If she didn't want him to finish hanging up the lanterns, there was nothing to get in their way.

Taking his hand, Stevi began to draw him away from the ladder and toward the beach. She wanted him for herself for a little while especially since something was telling her that this could all go away before she knew it.

But as she began to draw him toward the beach, he said, "Wait, don't you want to put everything away first?" She looked at him as if she didn't know where he was going with this. "So that nothing gets stolen," he explained.

She laughed softly and shook her head. "This is Ladera. Nothing ever gets stolen here."

"Yeah, right," he said, humoring her. Every place had some sort of threat of theft to reckon with. Ladera wasn't some fairyland and for the most part, people always acted on their worst impulses—at least they did in his experience.

"No, really," she stressed, putting her hand on his wrist. "This has to be one of the safest towns in the country. People trust one another here. Nobody locks their cars or their houses. And everyone looks out for everyone else," she added. "We've got a police department, but frankly, they're just for show." At least that was the conclusion she had come to. "That and for finding lost pets and an occasional kid who wanders off."

"Like your nephew?"

She laughed. "What's Dad been telling you? Ricky has more energy than any two kids put together and if one of us isn't watching him 24/7, he tends to get bored and goes off exploring—not always where he can be all that easily found."

"He wandered away from your father when Richard was talking to that guy."

"Who?" she asked idly.

"Crenshaw, I think his name was," he said, watching her reaction. What he hoped to learn he wasn't sure, but maybe there was something to be gotten out of this simple exchange. "Know him?"

"You mean Larry Crenshaw?"

"That might have been his name," he allowed, feeling that if he came on too intensely, he might alert her to the real reason he was probing her for information.

"He and Dad have known each other for years, and I think Dad said he's a native to the area—just like Dad. From what I can see, Larry's not a good friend of Dad's or anything, but they do go way back. I think they were in high school together. Frankly," she said, lowering her voice as they walked, "I'm glad he's not one of Dad's good friends."

He was instantly alert. Maybe this was something he could use. "Why?"

Maybe she was being unfair to the man, Stevi thought. But he made her flesh creep sometimes. "Nothing I can put my finger on, but there are times when he seems kind of, I don't know, icky."

He gave her a highly skeptical look. "That's not a really very helpful description unless you're talking about something that you just stepped in or that just melted."

Stevi shrugged. Ordinarily, she didn't like talking against anyone. But there was something off-putting of late about her father's onetime friend. "I've caught him looking at times."

"What do you mean, 'looking'?" Mike asked. "Looking at what?"

"At me, at Alex, at Cris and Andy. He used to be a really nice guy, but in the last couple of years, he's been different. There's something in the way he looks at you that makes you want to take a shower."

How had they gotten on this topic? Crenshaw and his creepy stare was *not* what she wanted to talk about tonight.

"Oh, don't mind me," Stevi told him in her next breath. "I'm probably just imagining it." She rolled the thought over in her head and decided she didn't want Mike thinking that she was delusional. "But I have to confess that I'm glad he doesn't come around much. He just comes by to check things out."

The tide was coming in and the water

flirted with the edges of their shoes as they walked along.

"Check what out?"

"If anyone's got any complaints, anything gone missing, things like that. Most of the time, the guest has just misplaced whatever it is they think is missing. But it gives Larry something to chase down. I think he wanted to be a cop in Los Angeles and he just couldn't make the cut. Ladera isn't exactly the liveliest place if you crave action and I think Larry really does." As far as she was concerned, they'd spent more than enough time on Larry Crenshaw and his mode of operation. "Why are we talking about him, anyway?"

Mike shrugged off the question. "No reason. Ricky said he thought Crenshaw was boring and that just made me curious."

"Okay, explanation accepted," she teased. "While we're at it, you have any other questions you need answered?"

He slanted a glance at her before asking, "Now that you mention it, there is one, but it's not about Crenshaw."

Even better, she thought. She didn't want to waste the evening talking about the police officer. "Shoot," she said.

"Why did you stop running?"

She wasn't sure what she was expecting, but it wasn't this. She wasn't sure she'd even heard him correctly. "Excuse me?"

"That first morning we met," he elaborated, "you were running along the beach. That's something people usually do on a regular basis. But you haven't been running since I landed on your beach. I was just wondering why."

Before she answered that, she had a question of her own.

"How did you know I was running?" she asked. "You weren't conscious when I found you. Your eyes were definitely shut and it took me a couple of minutes to get you to respond, so how did you know I'd been running?"

"I felt the rhythm. You were running

and coming toward me at a steady pace. I could feel every one of your footfalls telegraphing themselves through the wet sand."

He'd been lapsing in and out of consciousness and he had realized that? "I'm impressed."

"Don't be," he told her. "The mind does funny things to you when you're at death's door."

The phrase brought with it a very real shiver down her back. "I'd rather not think about you being at 'death's door,' thank you."

He didn't dwell on her response. It would only take him in a direction he'd already barred himself from taking.

"Nevertheless," he told her, "that's where I was. At death's door. If you hadn't come along, I would have died. You saved my life."

The phrase made her smile. She'd never been so glad to have been in the right place at the right time. "You know, in some ancient cultures, my saving your life would mean that your life was mine to do with as I wanted."

"And if it was," he asked her, "if my life was yours to do with as you wanted to, what would you do with it?"

"Easy. I'd set you free," she said without hesitation. "The only thing one person should own of another is their heart."

He laughed softly. "Now, there's a romantic notion."

She smiled up at him as she felt that warmth that only he could create spreading inside her. "I suppose that it is."

Mike looked at her for a long moment, hopelessly tempted to recreate that wondrous, singular moment from the first time they walked together on the beach when his lips touched hers.

But he held himself in check, knowing that to give in wouldn't be fair. Not to her.

So he did what he could to hold himself at bay, tamping down the desire that kept insisting on rising to the surface.

What surprised him was how hard that was to do.

A good deal harder than it should have been. Emotions used to be nonexistent for him. That wasn't the case anymore.

"You didn't answer me," he said.

Was that her heart beating so hard? Stevi wondered. It was almost as if she was waiting for something to happen, something to sweep her away from this reality to another, far more tender world.

"About what?" she asked him quietly.

Why was it so hard to keep his mind focused on what he was saying? Why did he keep envisioning taking her in his arms, losing himself in her kiss? He was acting like some lovesick puppy, not the hardened law enforcement agent he was.

"About why you stopped running," he finally said.

"You," she told him, breathing out the word.

That didn't make any sense. "You stopped running because of me?"

She nodded, then jumped when the cold water came rushing back to shore again, overlapping her feet as it went.

"Yes," she answered.

Mike shook his head. "I don't understand. I didn't ask you not to run. I don't have anything to do with your running," he pointed out, unable to follow the logic she'd used.

"Yes, you do," Stevi countered, then explained to him how the process worked so that there would be no doubt in his mind.

"If I'm running, I can't spend that time with you. And the first couple of weeks you were here, you needed a lot of care, a lot of looking after. I couldn't ask anyone else to do that. I didn't want anyone else doing that," she confessed.

He looked at her, surprised by the intensity in her voice and further surprised by what she said next.

"You were my responsibility and I *wanted* to be the one taking care of you. Then, after you got back up on your feet—" she shrugged "—I just wanted to spend time with you—and who knows how much time I have to do that? Running isn't going anywhere," she added glibly. "I can always pick it up."

And I am going somewhere.

He couldn't tell but there was something about Stevi's eyes, eyes he'd initially thought seemed so unworldly-looking and innocent, eyes that told him she saw beyond his words.

She was a great deal wiser than he'd given her credit for.

Mike cupped her cheek before he realized what he was doing. But there was something within him that was prompting him, whispering that his window of opportunity would be closed soon and then he wouldn't be able to look at her like this, wouldn't be able to touch her and inhale the scent of her skin, of her hair. Wouldn't be able to enjoy the sensations that proved he wasn't as dead as he believed himself to be.

But still, he couldn't lead her on, couldn't allow Stevi to feel that he was someone she could count on, not even to be there for another day, much less be there forever.

"I'm not any good for you, Stevi." The words felt rough, dry against his tongue as he uttered them.

Rather than meekly withdraw, she took exception to what he told her.

"I'm old enough to make up my own mind about that," Stevi replied. "And I think, despite everything you might think about yourself, that you *are* a good man. Deep down inside, where it counts, you're a good man," she repeated with feeling.

"You can't say that," he told her, agonizing over the decision he had to make. Agonizing over leaving her. "You don't know me."

"Oh, I know you better than you think, Mike Ryan," she insisted. "For instance, I know that right now, you want to kiss me, but you won't because you don't think it's fair to me."

Her laugh was soft, sweet. Stirring.

"What you don't realize is that it's your *not* kissing me that isn't fair to me. Because I want you to kiss me. I want you to kiss me very much."

Because he knew in his heart that it would be the last time that any of this could happen, Mike brought his lips down to hers and kissed her.

He was kissing her goodbye.

CHAPTER NINETEEN

BECAUSE HE'D LEARNED to live by his instincts, Mike had never been one to ignore a gut feeling.

Right now, although he didn't want to admit it, much less listen to it, his gut was telling him he was playing with fire. That staying here at the inn for another day, for even another hour, was nothing short of asking for trouble.

Whatever supply of good luck he had ever had, he'd used up just by surviving to this point. Being allowed to be part of Stevi's life and around her family went beyond being icing on the cake. It was a gift.

But if he hung around longer, Mike had a strong feeling he would regret it. Not because staying here would change him—

it already had to an extent—but because staying here would just possibly change *them,* the people he had grown to care about. If something did happen to any of them because he was here, he wouldn't be able to live with the guilt.

So, in the tradition of the "better safe than sorry" school of thought, Mike knew he had to go.

Go without saying anything because if he did, if he sought Stevi out to tell her goodbye, something told him that he wouldn't be able to go. He just wouldn't be able to reach the door. The look in her eyes would hold him in place, especially since he really didn't want to leave.

It seemed ironic. For the first time in his life, he felt as if he had found a home. And to keep that home intact, he had to leave it.

But he couldn't go without at least leaving Stevi a note. Otherwise, she might think something had happened to him and she'd go out looking for him. That was the kind of person she was. She had to be informed that he was leaving and wouldn't be back.

So, with a sadness that felt heavier than any other emotion he'd ever felt before, Mike took out the pad and pen from Stevi's desk drawer and he began to write.

Wishing with all his heart that he didn't have to.

RICHARD GLANCED UP from his desk when he heard the knock on his office door. Before he could say a word in response, the door opened.

A feeling of déjà vu washed over the owner of the inn.

"Twice in two days, Larry. The law enforcement business that slow these days?"

The police officer strode in. Unlike the day before, Crenshaw walked into the office with purpose rather than just strolling in. Richard's smile was tight, forced, as the policeman looked at him.

"Actually, the exact opposite is true," Crenshaw said. "I'm here officially, Richard."

Richard took off his reading glasses and looked more closely at the other man. "That sounds ominous. Should I be worried?"

Instead of laughing the question off, Crenshaw appeared to be regarding it seriously. The expression on his face was somber.

"That depends," Crenshaw said as he stood in front of the desk. Reaching into his uniform breast pocket, he extracted a copy he'd made of a photograph and placed it, facing Richard, on the desk. "Have you seen this man?"

Richard found himself looking down at a slightly blurred photograph of Mike Ryan. For just a second, his breath backed up in his lungs. The next moment, he was breathing regularly again.

"What's he done?" he asked quietly, still regarding the photograph closely, as if he was studying it.

"He's a drug dealer." Crenshaw left the photograph on the desk, as if he thought that the longer it was viewed, the more likely a connection would be remembered. "Might actually be high up in the organization chain of command." Crenshaw raised his eyes to study Richard carefully. "Word has it he was spotted around here, at the inn. Know anything about that, Richard?" he asked very deliberately.

Richard raised his eyes from the photograph and looked at the man he had known, marginally, for most of his life. There was something in Crenshaw's voice that made him feel uneasy. But not uneasy enough to blurt out what he had a feeling Crenshaw was waiting to hear.

"Can't say I do." He pushed the photograph back toward the police officer. "I haven't seen him."

STEVI COULDN'T FIND him anywhere, either on the premises or on the inn's grounds. He wasn't working on the decorations, wasn't in his room or in any of the common areas.

She didn't know why, but that made her

uneasy, like someone on the verge of an anxiety attack—although she really didn't know what that felt like since she'd never had one before.

She supposed she was just being paranoid. After all, it wasn't as if the inn comprised only a few rooms, the way it had when it first opened its doors over a hundred and twenty years ago. Thanks to a number of expansions over the years, the inn had more than thirty-one rooms and two common areas.

Granted, Mike wouldn't have been in most of the rooms because those were for the guests and blessedly, this time of the year, the inn was operating at maximum capacity.

They could play hide-and-seek for the rest of the day without their paths ever crossing.

She sighed. It was a daunting thought. However, because she believed in beginning at the beginning, Stevi headed to her room, which was still *his* room at this point as far as she was concerned.

Reaching the room for a second time in less than an hour, Stevi knocked hard, then used the side of her fist to bang harder.

Nothing.

Maybe he just wasn't answering the door, she thought, frustrated.

At least she could satisfy herself with eliminating the room as a possible location for Mike. That way she could go on to look for him elsewhere.

Methodically.

It was as good a plan as any.

Taking out her key, Stevi inserted it in the lock, took a deep breath and then turned it very slowly, giving Mike, if he *was* there, ample time.

"I'm coming in, Mike," she announced loudly—and found herself talking to no one.

He wasn't there.

"Drat," Stevi murmured under her breath. *Where was he?*

Turning to leave again, she noticed something on top of the covers on the bed.

Drawing closer, she realized that what she was looking at was a note.

Her heart stopped.

Anticipating the worst, she felt tears pooling in her eyes as she picked it up. She almost couldn't bear to read it, but she knew she had to. The sooner she forced herself to read it, the sooner she could decide what to do.

"I'm sorry," the note read. "It's better this way. Thanks for everything. You were great. Mike."

A wealth of emotions swirled around inside of her, colliding with a fierce amount of energy. It occurred to such a degree that she felt as if she was all but paralyzed.

And then, exercising an extreme amount of disciplined self-control, Stevi managed to snap out of it.

She was not going to accept this lying down. If for no other reason than to discount his stupid comment that his leaving was "better" this way.

Better for whom?

Certainly not for her—and not for him if even half of what he'd told her was true.

Stevi looked down at the note and realized she was crumpling it. She smoothed out the page, forbidding herself to cry.

She needed help.

The first person she thought of, now that she believed Mike had taken off, was her father. She had faith in him. He'd know what to do. And if he didn't, then he'd know someone who would know.

Stevi ran out of her room, not bothering to close the door.

"WRONG ANSWER, RICHARD," Crenshaw informed him dourly when he continued to disavow any knowledge of the man in the photograph. "I know for certain that not only is this guy staying here at the hotel, but you've taken him in the way you had those other losers who came to you, down on their luck."

"They're not losers," Richard said, taking offense for the people who weren't there.

The laugh was short and contemptuous as Crenshaw continued, "I always told you that taking in strays like that would come back to bite you someday. Well, this is someday, Richard. Unless you've changed your mind and can tell me where he is." Crenshaw's tone was low and menacing.

Richard was completely unfazed by the threat that the officer posed. "I don't put tracking devices on my people, Larry. They come and go as they please, whenever they want."

The police officer's fair complexion was turning an angry shade of red. "Another wrong answer. You're going to make me do something I don't want to do, Richard," he said, taking out his service pistol and pointing it at him.

"Put that away, Larry! You can't aim that thing at me—are you crazy?"

"Perhaps. This guy worth hurting someone over?" Crenshaw asked, his tone malevolent. "Your family, for instance? You really want to make me do this Richard? You'll regret it more than I will."

"You're really threatening me, aren't you?" Richard asked incredulously, hardly able to believe his own ears. He rose from behind his desk. "What's gotten into you, Larry?" he asked, his voice deep with anger.

The other man narrowed his dark brown eyes. "Don't patronize me, Richard. Everything's always gone your way but not everybody's got this Norman Rockwell life you cling to," Crenshaw said, making no attempt to hide his contempt. "Some of us live in the real world. Now, *where is he?* Tell me! I know you know."

"But I don't," Richard answered.

The next moment, Richard stumbled backward from the force of the punch the other man had delivered across his face.

Crenshaw pointed his weapon at him. "Want to try again?"

Just then, without pausing to knock, Stevi pushed open the door and hurried in.

"Dad, I have to talk to you, it's about Mike—"

Stevi came to a skidding halt when she saw the other man and the weapon he had in his hand. Her heart stopped when she saw her father's expression.

"What are you doing?" she demanded of the police officer at the same time that her father shouted a warning.

"Stevi, get out of here!" Richard ordered, but it was too late.

Crenshaw had already grabbed her by the arm and yanked her in. He kicked the door shut.

HE HADN'T SEEN very much when the door was opened, but what he had seen had made a huge impression on Ricky. Grandpa looked really upset and Aunt Stevi had cried out when that man he didn't like grabbed her and pulled her in.

He'd jumped when the door slammed.

Ricky thought of going in to help, to save his grandpa, but despite his bravery, he knew he was too little. He could bite the man, but maybe the man would shoot Grandpa or Aunt Stevi to get even.

He needed a grown-up.

Somebody who would listen to him.

Ricky ran to get his mother.

MIKE SHOVED HIS hands into his pockets. His right hand came in contact with something. Taking it out, he found himself staring down at the seashell Stevi had given him that night they'd walked along the beach.

His fingers curled around it. Mike blew out a breath and stopped walking.

He was taking the coward's way out.

And though he knew in his heart that this was the right thing to do, that disappearing out of their lives was for the best, he still couldn't force himself to do it.

Not because his life would be barren. He'd already resigned himself to that.

But he couldn't leave without at least warning them about Crenshaw, not when the man seemed to make a habit, according to Stevi, of turning up in Richard's life from time to time.

It wasn't just a hunch, he knew for a fact that the police officer was dangerous, that he was involved in the cartel's drug trade.

If he told Richard, the man would know what to do to protect himself and his family. For all he knew, the owner of the inn had contact with other police officials, honest officials, who could arrest Crenshaw or, at the very least, investigate him.

He couldn't leave without ensuring that the people he'd come to care about were safe.

Making up his mind, Mike slipped the seashell back into his pocket, turned around and began to head back to the inn, quickening his pace.

He was no longer just walking away, he was heading back with a purpose.

Mike had just walked in through the entrance and taken less than half a dozen steps toward the reception area when

Ricky flew into him, all arms and legs and panic.

Mike anchored him in place by putting one hand on the boy's shoulder. "Hold on there, little guy, who's chasing you?"

Breathless, Ricky gulping in air, his words came out almost disjointed. "Nobody...but he's...gonna...hurt Grandpa...and...Aunt...Stevi."

Mike froze. "Who's going to hurt them?" He collected himself and dropped to one knee to be at the boy's level. "What did you see?"

Still taking shallow breaths, Ricky spat out, "Aunt Stevi knocked on Grandpa's door and she walked in and the man grabbed her!"

It was hard for him not to shake the words out of the boy. Mike struggled for control as he asked Ricky, "What man?"

Taking another deep breath, Ricky managed to stop gasping. "The boring one. The one Grandpa was talking to yesterday. He's there in Grandpa's office. He's got a gun."

Mike was trying very hard to make sense of what the boy was saying. Icy fear scraped along his spine. He tried to tell himself that maybe the boy was mistaken. "That's because he's a police officer," he told the boy, trying his best to get Ricky to calm down. "They have guns on their belts."

But even as he said it, Mike knew the situation was a dire one. Exactly what he had feared was coming to pass.

"No." Ricky shook his head, swinging it from side to side, his hair flying half a beat later. "He was holding it," Ricky cried, his terror growing. "Pointing it at Grandpa!"

Mike's mind began to race.

Could Crenshaw have learned that he was alive and here at the inn? If he had, then he had to be desperate and desperate men did terrible, desperate things.

Taking hold of Ricky's shoulders, he looked down at him sternly and gave the boy instructions. "I need you to be brave, kid. Go to your mother, tell her what you told me." Cris was levelheaded, he thought. She'd do the right thing.

This time, Ricky bobbed his head up and down. "Okay. Are you gonna save them?" he said before he took off.

Mike squared his shoulders. "If I can, kid. If I can."

With that, he quickly strode around the side of the inn, hurrying to Richard's office. Had so much not been at stake, had it only been the other man and him, he might have attempted to get the drop on Crenshaw. To look in through the outside window and take the man down with one well-aimed shot.

Only problem was, his gun was somewhere in the middle of the ocean and he had no weapon.

Even if he did, if he could have gotten his hands on a gun, he'd be risking the two people in there with the police officer. If he managed to shoot Crenshaw first, the police officer could still fire as he went down, which meant that he could accidentally get one or the other.

He couldn't take that chance.

Couldn't risk either of them being hit.

There was only one course of action open to him that gave Richard and Stevi a chance of getting away. He had to make Crenshaw think he was surrendering.

If he could get close enough to him, he could either disarm him or block the shot with his body, allowing Richard and his daughter to escape.

Mike wasn't stupid, he knew that if he merely surrendered, no matter what Crenshaw threatened or promised, the police officer couldn't allow two witnesses to live. Mike knew what Crenshaw was thinking. He'd kill him first, then get rid of Richard and Stevi.

It couldn't go down that way.

Mike couldn't remember the last time he'd been scared, not even when he'd avoided the kill shot on the boat, but that was because he hadn't felt he had anything to lose. Life wasn't all that precious to him to begin with.

But he was scared now.

And the life that was precious to him now wasn't his own.

He reached the closed door of Richard's office.

"Crenshaw?" he called in a loud voice, through the door. "I hear you're looking for me."

"Ryan?" he heard the man reply. "Is that you?"

Psyching himself up, Mike leaned his forehead against the door, doing his best to visualize the right thing going down. "Yeah, it's me."

"Mike, run, he's got a gun!" Stevi screamed.

The next moment, Mike heard her cry out in pain. Crenshaw must have hit her. The thought enraged him.

"Leave her alone, Crenshaw!" he shouted. "It's me you want. I'm unarmed and I'm coming in."

"Slowly, Ryan," Crenshaw instructed, "or their blood's on your hands."

Mike strained to hear more discussion coming from the office.

"You're not going to be able to get away with this," Richard said.

"Let me worry about that," Crenshaw growled. And then his voice rose again. "You coming in, Ryan?"

Mike turned the doorknob slowly and eased the door open. He had one hand raised.

"Both hands!" Crenshaw ordered, aiming the muzzle of his gun not at him, but at Stevi. "Raise both hands in the air!"

"Watch where you aim that thing," Mike said quickly, doing as the other man instructed.

"I know exactly where I'm aiming 'that thing,'" Crenshaw retorted. There was a smile on his lips. "Welcome to the party, Ryan. Now get in here and shut the door behind you!"

CHAPTER TWENTY

HANDS STILL HELD up high over his head,
Mike moved away from the door. Crenshaw was standing to the side of Richard's desk, maximizing his vantage point
so that he could see both of the hostages
he'd taken, and now, Mike, as well.

When Mike looked at Stevi, he didn't
see fear so much as anger.

He had to get them out of here before
the entire situation got out of hand.

"Okay, I'm here," he said to Crenshaw.
"Now let them go."

The other man's smile indicated his
satisfaction. "It doesn't work that way,"
Crenshaw said.

That wasn't an answer Mike was willing to accept. "Look, these people never

did you any harm. It's me you want. Take me hostage, let them leave."

Crenshaw's smile vanished, as did his patience. "This is your fault," he snapped. "If you'd just died the way you were supposed to, none of this would have had to happen." And then he corrected himself as he waved the muzzle of his gun to include his initial two hostages. "None of this had to happen. But you forced my hand and now they've turned out to be witnesses."

"They won't say anything," Mike stressed. He looked at Richard. "Richard, tell him you won't say anything," he pleaded.

But rather than agree, the way Mike had expected him to, Richard shook his head. "I'm afraid I can't do that."

Was he *trying* to sign his own death warrant? His and Stevi's?

He turned to Stevi. "Stevi, talk some sense into your father."

"He is talking sense," Stevi replied, glaring at Crenshaw.

Mike's heart sank. He had to save their lives, but they weren't helping him any.

"See?" Crenshaw said to him, as if the responses proved some point of argument he'd made. "Not that I would have actually believed either of them if they'd sworn to take a vow of silence."

Mike tried another route, all the while watching for a sliver of an opening that would allow him to get the drop on the other man and take him down before he could do either Richard or Stevi any harm.

"You can't kill us here," he insisted. "Someone will hear the gunshots. Besides, how are you going to get rid of the bodies? You haven't thought this through," he said, trying to ruffle Crenshaw's thin veneer of composure.

"No, I haven't thought this through," Crenshaw agreed. The renewed expression of complacency was in direct contradiction to what Mike expected to see. "Not past you—and now them—being dead." The police officer's eyes narrowed into slits. "I had a nice little lucrative business going before you came and messed everything up. My partners have all pulled out, taken their trade someplace else," he accused. "So this—" Crenshaw waved his weapon from Stevi to her father and then back again "—is all on your head.

"The only thing left for me to decide is who goes first. You—" he aimed the muzzle at Mike, then swung over toward Richard "—or you. I always did hate your chipper Mr. Rogers attitude, Richard." Crenshaw's expression was dark and ugly. "It's easy being chipper when there's nobody telling you what to do, ordering you around as if you were a lackey." For a moment, he appeared caught up in some melodrama playing out in his head. Then he was pointing his weapon at Stevi. "Or you," he concluded.

Fear shot through Mike. "Leave her alone!"

Crenshaw swung his gun back to point at him. "Shut up! You're in no position to give orders."

Still aiming the weapon at Mike, Crenshaw dug into his back pocket and took out a muzzle extension to muffle the sound of the weapon being discharged. As he spoke, he attached the extension on to the end of the muzzle.

"By the time they find your bodies, 'Larry Crenshaw' will have disappeared." He laughed , the sound chilling Mike's blood. "Sounds like a happy ending to me."

"You won't get away with this," Stevi insisted. "Somebody'll hunt you down and make you pay."

"Maybe," Crenshaw allowed, although it was obvious that he thought the possibility was remote. "But it won't do any of you any good, now, will it?" he asked.

Mike had no doubt that the man swaggering before them was cold-blooded enough to carry out his threat. He also knew that there was no bargaining with him. If he were to take a guess, he would have said the police officer was relishing what he was about to do: to kill not just him, but Stevi and her father.

It would be making his worst nightmare come true.

Desperate, he came up with a fragment of a plan. Mike made eye contact with Stevi, then deliberately looked first to her father, then toward the door before shifting his eyes back to her.

"This is going to be a piece of cake," Crenshaw declared as he raised his weapon to fire.

Mike yelled, "Run!" as he launched himself directly at Crenshaw, cutting the short distance between them into nothing.

Startled, cursing, Crenshaw fired just as Mike tackled him. At the same time, a split second before both men crashed to the floor, another shot rang out.

As Stevi watched, Crenshaw screamed and sank to the ground with Mike on top of him.

Rather than run for the door, Stevi ran to him. "Mike, Mike, are you all right?" she cried, falling to her knees beside him.

"Talk to me, please," she begged. "Say something." Still kneeling, she attempted to turn Mike over onto his back so she could see if he'd been the one hit by the bullet.

His eyes were closed.

There was blood, so much blood, all over the front of his shirt. The sight of it and its implications terrified her.

"Mike, *say something!*" she begged again.

"Ow," he murmured just as Richard came around to his other side.

Her father took hold of him and slowly tried to raise him to his feet. "Steady now," Richard coaxed. "Let's get you off this so-called police officer."

Scrambling to her feet, Stevi swung around and grabbed the weapon that Crenshaw had dropped when he was tackled. Holding it with both hands, hands that weren't quite steady, Stevi aimed the gun at Crenshaw's chest.

"Don't move!" she ordered angrily.

With Richard's help, Mike had made

it to his knees. But that had taken all the strength he had, so he remained there, kneeling on the floor. He covered his fresh wound with his hands. Doing his best to rise above the pain, Mike looked at the other man.

"I don't think he can, Stevi," he told her. "I think he's dead."

But she kept the gun aimed just where it was. "He could just be pretending," she said despite the growing evidence to the contrary beneath him.

"Let's get you into a chair," Richard said, taking hold of Mike's elbow and making a second attempt to get him up onto his feet.

It was at that point that all three of them, from slightly different vantage points, saw the partially opened window behind Richard's chair.

And saw the man standing outside, on the other side of the window.

"Silvio," Stevi breathed in a stunned whisper of disbelief.

The gardener lowered the gun in his hands.

The door to the office burst open. The first one through it would have been Ricky had Cris not been holding on to him with both hands.

"Grandpa, Grandpa, are you okay?" he cried frantically, taking everything in at once.

Richard exhaled a huge sigh of relief. It appeared that his family had been spared. "I'm fine, Ricky." He put his arm around Stevi's shoulders and hugged her to him. "We're all fine." And then he realized he had to amend that statement. "Except for Mike here," he said in his next breath.

"It's just a flesh wound," Mike said, dismissing the gravity of the situation. When he looked out the window again, Silvio was gone.

"How did he—" Turning back to Richard and Stevi, Mike wasn't even sure how to phrase his question about the man who had come to his rescue.

But he didn't have to. Cris provided them with the explanation.

"When Ricky came running in and told me what was going on, I didn't think calling 911 would get anyone here fast enough, so I found Silvio." When her father looked at her quizzically, she added, "I've been paying attention, Dad. I knew he didn't exactly have a traditional background, so I took a chance that maybe what had brought him here all those years ago was something that could be used to help us now."

Mike heard sirens approaching.

"I sent him to you," Cris continued. "Then I called 911."

Only half listening—she could always get details later—Stevi put the gun on her father's desk and turned her attention to her hero.

"Let me see that," Stevi said. She took Mike's hands away from his wound to get a better look at it. It didn't improve from this vantage point.

The sirens grew louder, the sound becoming another entity in the room.

Richard's eyes shifted to Mike. "Do we need to hide you?" he asked, surprising everyone in the room, including Mike.

There was just the barest hint of a resigned, complacent smile on Mike's lips as he replied, "No. I'm not hiding anymore."

"Cris," Stevi addressed her sister without looking away from the wound, as if afraid that if she did, it would grow that much worse, "get me some clean towels, some peroxide—and Silvio," she concluded as the man, sans his weapon, walked into the by now very crowded office.

The gardener's dark eyes swept over the people in the room, doing a casualty count. They came to rest on the police officer on the floor.

"He's dead," Mike told him.

Silvio nodded, as if someone had told him a plant in the garden had failed to thrive.

"I know," he said in the same calm voice he always used.

Stevi looked at the man with ever growing respect. She knew by his statement—and by the way he carried himself—that he had to have been a man who always got what he aimed at. Had he been a sniper as well as a doctor? Whoever he had been in the life he'd led before he'd come to their doorstep, she was really glad that fate had brought him into their lives.

"He needs attention," she told Silvio, referring to Mike. Silvio nodded and turned toward her wounded hero, then paused as Stevi put her hand on his arm, drawing away his attention for just a moment. When Silvio looked at her quizzically, she said, "Thank you," with as much heartfelt sincerity as she could infuse in the two words.

Silvio grunted something unintelligible and nodded his head just as Cris returned with the supplies that Stevi had requested. Only then, as Silvio got down to work, did Stevi withdraw her other hand from Mike's wound.

She took a step back as the police officers, whom Cris had summoned by reiterating what her breathless son had told her, walked into the small office.

"DON'T YOU WANT to rest?" Stevi asked, not for the first time, concerned as Mike began to shrug into his shirt. Unlike the last wound he had sustained, this one, though it turned out to be less serious, necessitated his having to make use of a sling, thereby making even the smallest of chores—such as getting dressed—into a major undertaking.

Taking the other end of the shirt, Stevi helped him slip it on the one arm that could be put through the sleeve.

"I'm not an invalid, Stevi," he protested, wanting to do it himself.

"No," she agreed, "you're not. But it makes me feel better fussing over you just a little, all right?" she said. "Let me feel as if I'm a little useful in your life, at least for a couple of weeks."

You're more than a little useful in my life, he thought. *And that's just my problem.*

Giving in, Mike sighed and stopped struggling with the shirtsleeve and her.

"Knock yourself out," he told her. "And as for your first question, I'm really getting pretty sick of resting."

"Well, by my estimate," she informed him, "you haven't exactly been doing very much of it. After Silvio bandaged you up, you insisted on going down to the precinct to give the police a statement—"

"It was the right thing to do," he said, cutting in.

"No one's arguing with that," she pointed out, "but they were willing to give you a pass for a couple of days, especially after you gave them your superior's name and number and they verified your information. After all, it wasn't exactly as if Crenshaw was going anywhere but the morgue."

He didn't operate that way. His comfort was the least of his concerns.

"Better to get it all cleared up sooner than later," he said. "I wanted to make sure the police captain knew that none of what happened was in any way anyone at the inn's fault. What happened was between Crenshaw and me."

And, he added silently, he had also wanted to go to the precinct to make sure Crenshaw was the only one on that side of the badge who had been involved in the sale of the illegal drugs.

He'd come away satisfied that Crenshaw had been the only bad apple in the police station's barrel. He'd also noted that the precinct personnel had been appalled that one of their own had led such a double life.

Captain Reins told him that he was initiating an investigation right after the Fourth. That meant tomorrow.

"I noticed that in that statement you gave to the Captain, you covered for Silvio," Stevi said.

He began to shrug and realized that he couldn't, not without incurring shooting pains all up and down one side.

He made no apologies for not implicating the gardener. "Least I could do."

He knew that if Silvio's part in all this came to light, quite possibly the man's background might fall under investigation as well and he had a feeling that Silvio's past was best left untouched.

His shirt on, Mike fumbled with the buttons. Stevi pushed his hands out of the way and quickly closed all of them. With a smile, she smoothed down the front of his shirt.

Nodding his head, he said, "Thanks. Now, if you don't mind, I'd like to see the fireworks that everyone's been talking about, seeing as how I was the one to get everything ready for this big celebration of yours," he said.

"As I recall," she reminded Mike, "you did have a little help."

He paused and with his one good hand, he cupped her cheek as he looked down into her eyes. "As I recall," he countered, "I had a lot of help."

And then, ever so lightly, he brushed his lips against hers.

Stevi sighed. Her heart was racing again. He still had that effect on her and she had a feeling that he would for as long as he was in her life.

Which brought her to another point.

"Now that most everything's out in the open," she began as they walked out of the bedroom and into the hallway.

"Yes?" he asked when she paused.

She took his good arm and threaded it along her shoulders, then laced her fingers through his to keep him there. "Does that mean that you might be staying on a little longer?" she asked hopefully.

"It might…if I can find a place to stay."

She stopped walking to look at him, not sure if he was being serious or pulling her leg. "What do you mean 'if'? You've got a place to stay, right here."

He shook his head, dropping his teasing tone. "I can't keep taking your father's charity."

"It's not charity," she told him. "It's payback. You threw yourself on that monster's gun to save us. You've got a room here for life if you want it." Then, before he could protest, she added, "My father said so. Ask him if you want."

He wasn't disputing that, but there was another point he felt Stevi was missing. "That monster wouldn't have been here in the first place if it hadn't been for me."

She was not going to have this argument. "Don't split hairs," she said. "The bottom line is that you saved us and you can stay here for as long as you'd like to."

"What if I'd like to stay here on a permanent basis?" he asked.

She'd just started to head for the rear of the inn and she stopped walking again to face him, struggling to stifle the cry of excitement that was bubbling up in her throat, seeking release.

Was he serious? Oh, please, let him be serious, she thought.

It took everything she had not to squeal her words out. In the calmest voice she could muster, Stevi told him, "That can be arranged."

"You're sure?"

"I'm sure," she echoed.

"How sure?"

That was when she knew he was staying. She could feel every part of her singing.

"Oh, very, very sure. I've got an 'in' with the owner and I can put in a good word for you," she told him.

"Sounds good," he said with a nod. Then he swept her against him with his one good arm and kissed her one more time. "Now let's go see those fireworks."

"I think I already do," Stevi murmured happily as she led the way to the back lawn.

EPILOGUE

"I'M SORRY, I KNOW I haven't been down to talk to you for a while," Richard said, apologizing to both his wife and his best friend as he stood between their two headstones.

The two headstones couldn't have been more different. Amy's was all sleek, cool white marble with an angel on it, an angel whose face closely resembled his wife's the way she had appeared on their wedding day.

Dan's headstone, on the other hand, was just a basic headstone with no frills, no ornate carvings on it. It was simple and straightforward, like the man himself had always been. He had insisted on the headstone being almost nondescript and Wyatt, though resistant in the beginning, had finally given in and commissioned the headstone that his father had wanted to mark his grave.

"It's been pretty hectic here for a few days, as I know that you undoubtedly are aware," Richard told his audience of two. "And, as I know you're also aware, Stevi's decided she doesn't really want to go to New York or Paris or any of those other places she was considering after graduation."

His request to them to find a way to keep her home had obviously borne fruit, he thought happily.

"Seems that young man whose life she saved, the one you had wash up on our beach a couple of months ago, has her intent to stay right here with the family and the inn. And, of course, with him. With Mike."

He smiled as he sat on the seat that was built into the base of the tree next to their graves, thinking of everything that had happened since he'd last been to the small family cemetery.

"I really wasn't sure what to make of him to begin with. I know you two are looking after us, but I have to admit I had a few doubts about the way things were going to turn out. But it seems that Mike is an undercover DEA agent who'd spent more than two years infiltrating the American side of a drug cartel.

"Someone within our own Ladera Police Department found out about him and blew his cover—and almost his life—away. Mike was on a drug lord's cabin cruiser at the time and jumped overboard just when he was shot. If Stevi and Silvio hadn't brought him back to the inn and tended to his wounds, that boy would have been dead.

"As it is," Richard continued, still marveling that all this had happened to his family and to him, and that they were all alive to talk about it, "he wound up saving *our* lives, Stevi's and mine, because the inside man at the police department turned out to be none other than Larry Crenshaw." Richard shook his head, a chill running down his spine as he thought about the circumstances that were now behind him.

"You remember Larry Crenshaw, don't you, Amy? He was in high school with us and he was the one who was always trying to get you to go out with him, even though you were going with me. He had a king-size crush on you—and as it turned out, he never really forgave me for living what he felt should have been his life, or so he accused me. All this time and I never realized what kind of scum he really was.

"But Mike knew and he was willing to sacrifice himself to save Stevi and me. He might have died, too, if Silvio hadn't come to the rescue.

"That man never ceases to amaze me, Amy. He made your garden thrive, bringing all those dying plants to life. Turns out he knows how to do the same for people, as well as being one very impressive marksman."

He smiled at his wife's headstone. "I'm

pretty certain that you're the one responsible for bringing him to the inn in the first place. Always looking out for us, aren't you, darlin'?" he murmured.

"I suppose I don't really have to tell you the news, do I? But it does bear repeating, because it *is* such good news. With Larry's, let's say elimination, as a threat, that left a vacancy on the police force. Guess what? Mike interviewed for it—seems he's tired of undercover work—and easily got the job. Which is good because right after that, he turned around and asked our Stevi to marry him. You know what that means."

Richard chuckled, looking from one headstone to the other, as if waiting for someone to speak up. "Besides another wedding, it means that Stevi's staying put. She's decided to split her time between the art gallery in town and being the inn's event planner. My way of thinking is if she's going to be bossy, she might as well get paid for it, right?

"The first event Stevi's planning is her

own wedding. I'm not sure if that means she gets to boss herself around, or just how that's going to work, but we'll see."

He rose to leave, then stopped.

"Oh, I almost forgot. We're going to have two pairs of little feet running around just in time for Christmas. Seems Cris is pregnant, too. She didn't want to say anything until she started showing because she wanted Alex to enjoy the spotlight as long as possible. That's Cris for you," he said with a wide grin. "Always thinking of others. She's a lot like you that way, Amy.

"Cris's baby is supposed to be two weeks behind Alex's, and if I know Alex, it's going to be a competition right down to the wire. Since neither of the girls wanted to know what they're having, we're just dealing in neutral colors for now. Me," he confided, lowering his voice, "I'm hoping for little girls because we've done so well with the ones we were blessed with."

He beamed at Amy's headstone, recalling what it had been like during the early days, when they were overwhelmed and outnumbered parents doing the best they could.

He paused before turning back to walk up the incline to the inn. "Watch over them for me, you two. I could use all the help I can get. Well, I'd really better get going. I'll try to make it back sooner the next time. Until then, I'll trust you to keep everyone safe. Goodbye, my darling."

Kissing his fingertips, he pressed them to the angel on the headstone. "Goodbye, old friend."

With that, Richard turned toward the inn and began the climb back, thinking how very fortunate he was. The only thing that would have made him even more fortunate was if he could have had his wife and his best friend by his side, experiencing everything with him in the flesh rather than just in spirit.

But a man couldn't have everything, could he?

* * * * *

REQUEST YOUR FREE BOOKS!

2 FREE INSPIRATIONAL NOVELS
PLUS 2
FREE
MYSTERY GIFTS

Love Inspired
HISTORICAL
INSPIRATIONAL HISTORICAL ROMANCE